P A

D1591110

MARAUDER

During the bitter winter of 1862 the people of the Arkansas frontier were the all-too-easy victims of both Confederate guerrillas and Yankee renegades. Most feared of all was the crazed raider Cryson, who stained the land with the bloodtrails of his burning, thieving, murdering gang. Until one lone woman thundered out of the war-scarred hills to defend her home, to strike back against the raiders, to become the woman they called Marauder . . .

MARAUDER

During the bitter winter of 1862 the people of the Arkansas frontier were the all-too-easy victims of both Confederate guerrillas and Yankee renegades. Most feared of all was the crazed raider Crysop who stained the land with the bloodtrails of his burning, thieving, murdering gang. Until one lone woman thundered out of the war-scarred hills to defend her home, to strike back against the raiders, to become the woman they called Marauder . . .

C. H. HASELOFF

MARAUDER

Complete and Unabridged

LINFORD
Leicester

First published in the U.S.A. in 1982 by
Bantam Books, Inc.,
New York

First Linford Edition
published January 1987
by arrangement with
Bantam Books, Inc.,
New York, N.Y.

British Library CIP Data

Haseloff, C. H.
  Marauder.—Large print ed.—
Linford western library
I. Title
823'.914[F]   PR6058.A7

ISBN 0-7089-6342-0

Published by
F. A. Thorpe (Publishing) Ltd.
Anstey, Leicestershire
Set by Rowland Phototypesetting Ltd.
Bury St. Edmunds, Suffolk
Printed and bound in Great Britain by
T. J. Press (Padstow) Ltd., Padstow, Cornwall

To my students

Special thanks to:

Mr. and Mrs. Gus Edison
Dr. and Mrs. John W. Dorman
Joe Cavanaugh
Rita Anderson Bess

1

RHEA DAMERON sat under the flinty overhang, turning the apple against the keen blade of her knife. Slowly the ribbon of apple peel unwound and dropped into her lap. The blade cut against the pale yellow flesh, tipped in, and carried the first morsel to her mouth. She chewed. The tartness ran through her tongue, stimulating the juices. Again and again the knife bit into the delicate flesh and carried it silently to her mouth untouched by her hands. Rhea's eyes watched the distant hills and valleys, watched the fog, like smoke in the mountains' pockets, watched the sun work its way over the hills and shine weakly into the low valley. It was day again. The long winter night had passed.

Laying the apple core beside her, Rhea rose from the rocky ground and pulled the worn blanket about her shoulders over the coat of skin and fur she wore. She walked out of the cave, a shower of pebbles cascading before her. Oblivious to the slick treacherous footing, she

1

dared the earth to tangle her, to drop her to her knees. She walked along the path in a kind of daze, shoving the brittle grasping limbs aside with the sureness of purpose of Moses parting the Red Sea. Down through the rocks and brush, down from the bloody massacre where Dr. Isaacs, her father, and five wounded men, his patients, lay dead that December morning.

She took to the flat land along the creek and increased her pace even among the rocks that turned her ankles and ripped at her boots. Once she fell, tearing the flesh on the heel of her hand and sending pain unheeded up her arm. It was as if she defied her flesh, her mortality, and dared fate to take more from her that morning than it had already done.

Drizzle fell, coating, then freezing the bare trees that reached up and bent back on themselves like arthritic fingers; freezing the blown field flowers and weeds, the grey-yellow broom sage, the grass itself until it began to crinkle like broken glass under her feet. The silent wind played the icy limbs gently in their melodious shells, accompanying the snow that fell with a soft hiss to the frozen ground. Rhea refused to raise the blanket to cover her fur cap and hair. An icy crust formed on curls that strayed from the full blonde braid at the base of her small skull, on the spiky hairs of the cap, on the teary lashes surrounding her pale eyes. She stumbled again and rose again, walking faster until she reached the grove of persimmons and blackjack oak where the wounded cavalry horse stood. She mounted slowly settling into the saddle with a deliberate weight. Her spur dug into the animal's bony side, and it jumped sideways out of the grove and up the embankment.

The first time I ever saw her was from a window, a distant rider throwing herself and the horse against the storm. My sister and I watched her plunge into the icy creek, disappear, then reappear forty yards from our porch. "Get the gun," I said to Sarah as I kept watch. She returned barely able to drag the old front-stuffer shotgun Pa had left us. I capped and cocked it and propped it across my knee on the windowsill. We watched the rider dismount onto the porch and tie the horse to one of the support logs. She saw us in the window—two ragged hill children behind a cocked shotgun. And we saw her plainly—an ice woman, covered in fur, lithe, high cheekbones burned raw by the wind, just as ragged as we were. She watched us for a while, seeming to count our very hairs, deciding something, I thought. Then she opened the door I'd forgotten to lock. As I turned, she pushed the barrel up, and I discharged the old gun into the ceiling, blasting a clear hole and covering us all with dust and woody debris. The woman pulled the useless gun from my hands and set it behind her.

"I've come to take you home with me," she said. Her voice was firm. "Get your things. It's mighty cold, so wrap up."

"My pa said for us to stay here till he come home," I said.

"I talked with your pa, boy. He can't come home. You're to come with me now. He said plain you aren't to stay out here and starve for want of a pa or ma to care for you."

She lifted the kettle lid on the hearth. It was as empty as our bellies. Pa had gone to town four days ago for supplies. Sarah and me had finished what was left yesterday noon. And still Pa wasn't back.

"Move, boy. There's food and a fire on the other side of this day's journey."

I watched her kneel and begin going through

the box we kept food in. "You've come here to thieve," I said, knocking her to the dirt floor. "Thief! Thief!" I struggled with her, and Sarah came to help me. Once I kicked the woman, and she yelped. But mostly she only held us off, turning our blows aside with her palms, spinning us away and back until we spent our small strength against her. Then she pulled us to her tight. Sarah put her arms about the woman's neck and began to cry. I also wanted to cry, but was too big at ten.

"You're safe now," she whispered. "You're safe." We believed this woman we did not know.

"What are your names?" she asked us.

"John Luke Pierce," I said. "And this here's my baby sister, Sarah."

"My name is Rhea Dameron. You may call me Rhea."

After that we gathered up our clothes, Pa's gun, Ma's Bible, and the deed to our place. Rhea had me dig a hole in the sod floor by the hearth, and we buried our few valuables in the cook box and covered it over and packed it down.

Rhea led me and Sarah on the horse the remainder of that day across the snowy valleys

5

and hills. Sometimes she stopped the horse and rubbed our hands between hers or adjusted the blankets and quilts we'd brought from home around us. We ate the loaves of bread she had in her saddlebags, keeping them soft with our body warmth. Once when we stopped we made a little fire and warmed our feet.

At dusk, Rhea pointed toward the long wide valley where two creeks ran down from the mountain into a single stream. "That's Lord's Vineyard," she said. And Sarah and I looked with curiosity at the place which was to be our home. It was a fine place to my child's eye—a fertile valley with bottom land for farming, a new orchard, and a small grape vineyard high on the hillside. The white-painted board and batten house sat snuggly against the south slope of the hill. There was a good stone barn below the house with a creek running through the animal lots. And there was an ample garden spot neatly laid by for winter. The builder of the house had left some big trees about the yard so that it did not have the ravished look of a new homestead.

Rhea stood a long time looking at the scene. I guessed she was studying it, like Pa did our place when we'd all been to town. Sarah kicked me and it hurt, so I pinched her. Rhea looked back at us, ending further retaliation for the moment.

"My husband, Jamie Dameron, built this place," she said, and led the horse into the valley. I could see a faint light through the trees and felt the hope of it.

Rhea helped us down, unsaddled the horse and turned it into one of the straw-filled stalls. Then we walked together up to the house. When she opened the kitchen door the warmth of the room rushed us, shocking our brittle noses and fingers. A black woman was cooking supper, and the smell of hot biscuits made me dizzy.

"What have you brought home now?" she asked Rhea and came toward us.

We backed up against Rhea. Sarah and I had not seen a Negro but once before, when we came through Fayetteville on our way to settling our place. That Negro was a man, an old man bent and gray, who drove a white woman's carriage. Once after the war began, and I'd heard it was about Negro slavery, I'd asked Pa why folks wanted to fight a war for an old black man who drove a carriage. He'd looked at the fire a long time and said it was not just that, there was more to it—like stupidity and greed and pride, too. But this Negro was a woman and fairly young. She did not talk like the Negroes in the stories white men told. Nor did she hesitate to unwrap us or touch our little pink hides.

"They're nearly frozen, Rhea," she said, uncurling Sarah's red baby fingers. Rhea was unwrapping her scarf with one hand and carrying a wooden bucket to us with the other. The black woman pushed up our sleeves and gently put our freezing fingers into the warm water. Hot water on cold fingers hurts. She and Rhea rubbed our hands until the life began to come back.

"What's happening in here?"

I jumped at the voice, pulling my hand from the water and sloshing the Negro woman and Rhea. Suddenly I saw the most beautiful woman I had ever seen. Her auburn hair caught the lantern light, making little stars on the silky curls. Her eyes were a deep brown; her skin fair, almost translucent. The black mourning dress she wore set off her small waist and full bosom.

"Oh, I found these children and brought them home," Rhea said, smiling at us.

"There's barely enough food now," the pretty woman said.

"It will go a little further. Far enough to feed some little sparrows, I guess," the Negro woman said, as Rhea Dameron removed her cap and coat of skin and fur, and hung them on the peg by the door.

"Children," Rhea said. "It's time to get acquainted. This is Claudia Isaacs. She is my sister-in-law, my brother's wife. The other lady is Hillary Sanderson. Claudia, Hillary, our guests are John Luke and Sarah Pierce. They will be staying with us." The matter settled, Rhea smiled at us and led us to the table, pointing me into a chair and drawing up a high wooden stool for Sarah. The black woman set bowls of steaming stew and biscuits in front of me and Sarah. Rhea pushed the pot of honey closer.

Claudia Isaacs came to the table and took her seat. The pretty features were closer now and just as dazzling to my eyes. "My, but he does stare," she said. "Are you sure he's not half-witted? I won't have any idiots around my baby, Rhea. Heaven knows this house is informal enough. But I will not have that. I'll leave first."

I dropped my eyes quickly and tried to chew the half biscuit in my mouth. The doughy lump lodged in my throat and I began to choke, snorting and coughing and clawing. Finally it slipped down. Red-faced and moist-eyed, I took a long drink of water, seeming more an idiot, I thought.

"The little girl's so stringy, Rhea," Claudia said. "Wherever did you get such urchins?"

"The Pierce children are exceptionally bright," Rhea said. "They very nearly killed me this morning. And in a while we shall fatten them up, plump as spring lambs." Rhea sat down and took my hand. Hillary sat down, too. Pretty soon we formed a circle of hands and Rhea asked the blessing, thanking God for Sarah and me as though we were not burdens in that hard time of war.

We ate awhile, and Claudia seemed to forget us children. "Is Doctor Isaacs still with that sick family you took food to this morning?" she asked.

Rhea said nothing but sat with her elbows on the table and her fingers laced, looking down at her plate of untouched stew. "He's still there," she said. "But the news is not good. We'll have to discuss it later after the children are settled in." There was a pause and she asked, "How's Joey?"

"He's fine," Claudia said continuing her eating.

"Joey is Claudia's baby," Rhea said.

"He's really getting too big for me to lift," Claudia said. "Hillary spoils him. She takes him up every time he even whimpers."

Rhea Dameron watched her sister-in-law as she slowly broke and began to put honey on the burning hot roll. "Claudia, you'll have to overlook Hillary and me for a little while. Our nerves are not used to crying babies. Besides, babies need a lot of love. Sometimes that means a little spoiling."

"He's not your baby. You aren't always going to be around. I just wish one of you two little mothers could nurse him. Joseph was going to get me a wet nurse, you know. Even a cow would help."

"Joseph is, was," Rhea corrected herself, "very thoughtful. But, at least for a while, nursing should be good for you as well as the baby."

"That's easy for you to say. As long as Joseph was alive, I thought so; I surely didn't want another baby right away. But now he's dead. I can't see any benefit in it. I don't like it, and it's spoiling my figure."

"Spoiling your figure?" Rhea said softly. Her eyes swam with tears. "Life is certainly for the living. I'm glad you're adjusting so quickly, Claudia. My brother's been dead four whole days. You must have loved him a lot." Rhea stood up. "The children can have my stew, Hillary." Then she caught up her coat and went outside.

"I don't begin to understand her," Claudia said, breaking another biscuit. "She's the doctor's daughter, the physician's apprentice. She shouldn't be so emotional about death."

"She doesn't have your perspective, I guess," Hillary said, reaching for Rhea's bowl but losing the race to Claudia, who raked a good portion into her own bowl before dumping a spoonful on Sarah's plate and mine.

"I'm feeding a baby," she said, beginning to eat.

In a little while Hillary took us upstairs and got us ready for bed. I could see Claudia brushing that beautiful hair across the hall, but somehow it didn't shine so much.

"You say your prayers now and hop in bed," Hillary said, and we did. The sheets were warm from the warming pan she'd used. When Sarah went to sleep, I got back up and put on my britches and shoes. I wanted to talk to Rhea Dameron about my pa.

She wasn't in the house so I skinned out for the barn where I saw a light. I opened the door slowly and went inside. Rhea was sitting on a keg near the lantern. Her coat was thrown over the stall where the horse stood. She'd pulled her shirt tail out, and I could see the large black bruise on her ribs where I'd kicked her that morning. She was washing it, and it must have hurt because she winced. I stepped forward, and she looked up.

"Boy, it's too cold out here without your coat."

"Nah, I'm used to it. I'm tough," I said, already beginning to shake because of my dash from the house to the barn.

She pulled her shirt down, stood up, and tossed me her coat. "Put that on while I finish up. Then we'll walk back to the house together."

I took the coat. It came past my knees, warming me with her warmth, smelling slightly of the herbs and spices of her closet. Rhea removed a poultice from the horse's shoulder.

She washed the area and talked to me over her shoulder. "I took out the bullet," she said. "She was shot at the Battle of Prairie Grove, Arkansas. December 7, 1862. But it was in there awhile, so the heat in the poultice is needed to draw out more of the poison and fester. It makes her feel better, too."

"Is my pa dead?" I asked.

She turned around and looked right at me. "Yes," she said. "He was killed this morning. Your pa told me where to find you before he died."

I turned away so she wouldn't see the tears. I was beginning to shake pretty hard from the cold and now there was the shock of Pa being gone. "How'd it happen?" I choked a little in the asking. She took me by the shoulder and turned me toward her. "I ain't crying," I said.

"I know," said Rhea Dameron. "But it hurts pretty bad anyway. My father died today, too, so I know. And after a while, when I can be by myself in the night, I'm going to cry. I don't think that would hurt. Crying draws the poison out and makes you feel better. It's not crying that's wrong, John Luke. It's giving up. And after I cry, I can think better what to do about all of us."

14

"Is that boy out here?" Hillary said, coming in the door and pulling her shawl together. She saw us then, me standing in Rhea's coat and Rhea kneeling in the straw. "It's too cold out here for real talk," she said gently. "Come in the house."

Rhea stood up and took the lantern. We walked back to the house through the biting winter wind. The stars had bright little flares around them from the tears in my eyes.

"What happened to Pa?" I asked in the kitchen.

"Let's sit down first," Rhea said. I took a seat at the table. Rhea sat where she had sat at dinner and folded her hands on the table. Hillary brought over a few of the biscuits that were left and some honey. But I didn't feel like eating. Then she sat down, too, and told me about the dying at Eden's Bluff and how it came to happen.

"Your pa was conscripted," Rhea said. "By the Confederate Army of General Tom Hindman."

"But my pa was a Union man," I protested.

"A conscript is someone who serves against his will, John Luke. Your pa did not want to join the Confederates, but he was forced to.

15

Claudia's husband was, too. The conscripts were rounded up and taken with the army to Prairie Grove. They were thrown into the fight against General Blunt's army from Missouri. Many of them died there at the peach orchard, like my brother, Joseph. They refused to shoot the Union men, yet their Confederate officers threatened to kill them if they did not. So they loaded their rifles with powder and wadding and tamped them down. But the officers did not know the men did not put in the shot. Those men dropped their minie balls and bullets on the ground around them. Then they ran yelling and firing at Blunt's soldiers with blank guns. Blunt's men didn't know. So a lot of the conscripts died rather than fire a deadly shot against the Union. I don't know of more courage than that, or a sacrifice greater than a man's life. Your father was with those men, John Luke. It's your courage, too, your heritage from him.

"But you have another gift from your father —he remembered you and Sarah. When the fighting let up, though he was wounded, he tried to get home to you. He stopped to rest in a barn with some other men. A Confederate patrol found them and shot them down. Later,

16

other men found them and hid those who were still alive in a cave at Eden's Bluff. My father doctored them. But this morning they were found and killed. Five wounded men and my father. I went there to take my father supplies and discovered their bodies. Your pa held on to life long enough to save you—to tell me how to find you and to give you to me. He loved you and Sarah very much. You must always know that. But for his love, you were dead. Your lives are very special. God has a special plan for you both."

So Rhea Dameron gave me the news of my father's death. But she also gave me his courage and love and a sense of purpose for my life, although I did not know then what that purpose was. Sarah and I grew up on Rhea's sustaining story of Eden's Bluff conscripts. It was a long time before I knew the whole story of the four days in early December 1862—what it meant in Rhea's life, and how it joined our lives forever.

2

THE next morning, Rhea Dameron and I drove from Vineyard to the cave at Eden's Bluff. It was not so much she let me go as I would not stay behind. I was, after all, my father's son. After what he'd done for me, nobody could keep me from getting him.

We left just before daylight. Our wagon bounced and rattled all morning across the roadless country. The sun was nearly overhead before we reached the menacing bluff. Two other wagons sat in the flat land above the creek. Rhea and I walked up to the cave where Pa was killed. A group of men under the overhang near the mouth of the cave stood with their hands thrust deep in their pockets. Their noses were red from the biting cold. Their breath made frosty patches on their mustaches and beards. None of them smiled at us. They seemed sullen and studied us with hard, suspicious eyes.

Nobody said anything, so Rhea and I went inside. We stood there in the entrance, letting our eyes grow accustomed to the light. I could see bodies lying along the wall covered with blankets. Some had the blankets tied about them. I thought they looked like pieces of meat Pa wrapped for the smokehouse. Three men worked over the body of one soldier, but when they saw us they stopped. One came toward us.

He took off his cap. I could see the perspiration on his bald scalp, plastering the thin hair over his ears against his head. "Missus Dameron," he said. "I'm mighty sorry about the doctor. Ain't a family hereabouts won't feel his loss." He seemed uncomfortable. "Most folks sent somebody for the bodies. Why didn't your brother come for him, ma'am?"

"My brother died at Prairie Grove," Rhea said evenly. "Mr. Gilstrap, I have a wagon below, but I need help getting my father and the boy's father down."

Gilstrap suddenly noticed me. He studied me. "We don't know the man yonder. Do you know it's the boy's father?"

"I know," she said. "He told me where to find the children."

"You was here?" Gilstrap asked. The other two men were listening now.

"I was here to help my father and to bring supplies," Rhea answered.

"Guess you don't know who tipped off the killers do you, ma'am?" one of Gilstrap's men said.

"They were alive when I left night before last," said Rhea.

"You know Blackie Foard, Missus Dameron?" Gilstrap asked.

"Yes. He brought my father and me here. I understand he and his brothers carried the wounded men up here for their safety."

"Wasn't very safe, was it?" one of the other men said.

"Ma'am, we ain't questioning you. Your pa died here. But after the hunters found the bodies. Blackie Foard lit out. We know somebody told who was in the cave and where it was. These men here was our friends, our family," Gilstrap said. "We aim to know who told."

"I don't know who told, Mr. Gilstrap, but Blackie Foard wasn't the only one who knew where this cave was. While I was here someone whistled, and he went to them. When he came back he had quilts and food. He said their families brought it."

"Blackie Foard's a dead man far as I'm

20

concerned," a man back in the shadows said. "His body'd be up here with the dead ones if he was honest."

"Maybe he was on an errand when it happened," Rhea said. Nobody answered her. "Why would he save, then betray them?" she asked.

One of Gilstrap's friends spoke. "The Foards was never friends with the Grahams. Billy and Frank, Jr. are dead over there."

Rhea started to speak but stopped. "We'll help carry your folks down," Gilstrap said. They called another man, and the four of them took Pa and Dr. Isaacs to the wagon for us.

Rhea and I drove from there into Prairie Grove. It was a spent town. Spent by the battle. Spent emotionally by the conflict, defeat, and grief. The town seemed empty as we came down the street in the late afternoon. When we pulled up by the undertaker's place, Jesse Branch and two Union soldiers were standing on the porch.

"No need to get down, Missus Dameron," Branch said. "I ain't got a coffin or a tear left. There ain't neither one anywhere in town." Rhea sat back.

21

"Can you help me with the grave?" she asked.

"Bury your own dead, lady," one of the soldiers said. "There ain't no help here." Branch didn't say anything. He ducked his head and went inside.

Rhea slapped the horses' backs with the reins. They stepped off toward the Cumberland Presbyterian Church. There we were to bury the two men we carried, beside the fresh grave of Rhea's brother and old grave of her mother in the churchyard. It started to rain before we reached the little shed where the gravedigger lived. Rhea knocked on the old man's door, but he didn't respond. Finally she shouted out, "Jed, I know you are in there! Open the door!"

"Go away," a thick voice said.

Rhea pounded some more and tried the door latch. Still he did not come. Finally she walked back to the wagon and stepped up on a spoke to get on the box. She looked at the canvas thrown over the two bodies as she climbed, and suddenly she jumped down. She said something to herself and went back to the door. I saw her reach under her coat and pull out a shining Colt .36 pocket pistol. A moment later, she shot the lock off the door and pushed it open. The next

I knew, the old gravedigger staggered out with his finger still stuck in the handle of a jug. She shoved his hat on his head and carried his coat.

"Get the shovel," Rhea said. He seemed to have lost track of his mission and started back to the sheltering shack. Rhea put a shot squarely through the jug's bottom, exploding the bottle and liquid into the air and soaking Jed's pants. "Get the shovel," she said softly. Jed shook the busted bottle neck from his finger and started toward the tool shed past Rhea. He cussed loud, not caring for her ears or mine. She tossed him his coat.

While the drunken gravedigger laid out the four weathered boards that defined the grave and pinned them together with their rusty pins, I stood on the stone curb of the plot watching the rain, counting the fresh hills of dirt in the little cemetery. Rhea made me get in under the wagon for shelter. Jed laid a canvas to the side of the grave and began to methodically cut the sod, tossing it on the sheet. He dug steadily with the long narrow shovel, piling the dirt higher and higher, until he stood hip deep in the muddy hole. He got out, stuck the shovel in the ground, and started to the wagon. Rhea stepped in front of him, holding the pistol in his belly.

"It isn't deep enough," she said. "Dig it deeper, please."

Jed returned to the hole and dug. In a short while he was no longer visible, but we could hear him muttering, cussing to himself. When he raised himself out of the slippery muck finally, he smiled.

"Run to the shed and get me some ropes, boy," he said. I looked at Rhea, and she nodded. "We can put 'em both in the same hole for now," I heard him say as I started for the shed.

By the time I got back, Jed was red-faced and spitting, just starting the second grave. I guessed Rhea didn't approve of a single grave. She stood at the end of the first hole, looking at the sky. It was getting dark. "Can I help you dig, Jed?" she asked.

"The day I need a hardheaded, pistol-toting, smart-mouth woman to help me dig, I'll turn in my shovel and climb in my own hole," he said.

"Dig faster then," Rhea said.

Jed dug steadily, tossing dirt up beside the grave. When it was deep enough, he climbed out. He and Rhea went around to the back of the wagon. I heard them splitting and cutting the canvas that covered Pa and Dr. Isaacs. They wrapped the canvas around the blanket-wrapped men and tied it. Then they carried the bodies one at a time to the graves and laid them on top of the ropes. Jed worked one side of the ropes and Rhea and I held a rope apiece on the other. Slipping and staggering in the mud, the three of us struggled to lower the men into their graves. My fingers were nearly frozen. The ropes slipped through them till I caught a loop around my hands. I slipped onto my seat trying to hold the weight.

"Be careful, dammit!" Jed said to me.

"The boy's doing the best he can," Rhea said.

She strove against the weight in the slick footing, too. I thought I saw blood on the rope when it slipped in her hand, but she didn't say anything. Her skirts were wet, covered with mud as she waded across the cemetery plot and picked up a shovel. She stood on the muddy dirt mound and helped Jed cover the bodies. Pretty soon the graves were just knolls of red mud, and we were three whipped people in an empty world of cold rain and mud and darkness

—a woman, a boy, and a drunken gravedigger who didn't want to be there. In the winter of 1862 nothing came easy. Everything was hard. Nature herself was against us.

"Well, ain't you going to whine out some words over the deceased?" Jed asked. "Sanctify the dead?"

"The boy and I know these good men are with God. It's not for us to sanctify them. We'll say our words in our hearts and not trouble you any further."

Rhea paid Jed for his work, his lost whiskey, and his door. He didn't ask for any of it, but she remembered it all. When Jed went off toward town to buy another jug, I didn't figure we owed him anything.

Rhea and I climbed in the old farm wagon and sat there a minute looking at the graves in the darkness and rain. "John Luke," Rhea said. "Nothing you ever do will be worse than this." She turned to the team and tapped them lightly until we moved off.

Rhea and I could not have reached Vineyard that night. We were too tired, and it was too far away in that rain and snow. We stopped the night at Doctor Isaacs' house. Rhea had grown up there so she knew her way around. Pretty soon we had a good fire going in the little sitting room.

She found us some old clothes and heated water to wash up in. We ate what we found and what was left of what we'd brought with us. Neither of us was too hungry. Rhea gathered some blankets and quilts. She made me a thick soft pallet by the fire and herself a bed on an old horsehair couch. We put lots of wood by the fireplace and blew out the lamp. But lying there in the firelight I was wide awake—too anxious to sleep, wanting to hold the day in my mind. Rhea felt the same, I guess, because when I wanted to talk she listened.

I told her about Pa, and what I remembered of my mother. I asked her a lot of things I didn't understand about war and conscripts. I knew there was a story the grown-ups shared that I did not understand. I saw that in the suspicious looks at the cave. I heard it in the men's voices. Even then I knew Rhea Dameron was no ordinary woman, that the four days that changed Sarah's and my life had changed hers, too. Somehow the streams of our lives had run together. The current had taken us and would not let go. That night in the dark parlor before the fire, Rhea Dameron finally told me about

Prairie Grove and its aftermath—about the four days that changed us and joined us close as blood.

3

HINDMAN'S Confederate troops were pulling back along the Van Buren Road. From her hiding place, Rhea could see the blankets wrapped around the canons' wheels to muffle the nocturnal retreat. She saw spent men hurling themselves against a mired caisson as other haggard men filed around to the left. There were men in Joseph Isaacs' farmyard drinking the water that flowed from the spring. During or after battle there was never enough water. Thirst parched the men's throats as they fell on their bellies beside the running stream and drank with their sooty faces pushed into the cold, living water.

"Get up! Make room for the next man!" Rhea heard the sergeant say as he forced men away from the water. "Move on. Move on, boys." The men drank slowly and went on.

The doors to Joseph's house stood open. Rhea had left them closed and locked that morning as she'd stolen away Claudia and Joey from the roadside farm and taken them to

Vineyard. Scavengers and layabouts had done their work while the soldiers fought. The women had saved but little and their lives in fleeing before the army.

Rhea left the hill, cut across a gulley, and began to parallel the road, struggling against the main current of the army in the thick under-brush and rocks. She watched the line of soldiers closely, looking for Joseph or her father, ready to use the pocket pistol hidden in her shirt.

A man walked out of line. Her grip tightened on the pistol. He stared a long time in her direction. She was sure he saw her, and she froze. He straightened, dropped to his knees, then fell onto his face in exhaustion. He snored with his head pillowed in the rocks, unmindful of the pain.

Rhea knew the truth then. The soldiers were totally spent, walking in their sleep, staggering under the weight of march, battle, and retreat. She saw now that discretion did not matter. She could make better time along the road, looking for her family. Rhea walked among the men, between them, against the flow of glazed eyes and begrimed, bewhiskered faces.

"Andy!" she shouted, reaching out to one

man she recognized. "Andy Potts!" Potts' place joined Joseph's on the south. Like Joseph, he'd tried to stay out of the fighting. She held the man's arm. "Andy, have you seen my brother? Joseph Isaacs? My father?"

Potts searched his numbness and found Rhea holding him. "Joe and me was with conscripts. He went down at the peach orchard," he said.

"Is he dead?" Rhea asked.

"I don't know, Missus Dameron. I just don't know," Potts said. She released him, and he staggered on up the long hill.

Rhea moved quickly through the men. She stepped onto a rock and surveyed the line coming along the road. Below her she saw Aggie Singpiel pulling on an abandoned horse. The animal was too near dead to respond to the fat little woman's tugging.

'It's exhausted, Mrs. Singpiel. The horse is done in, or they wouldn't have left it," Rhea said, trying to pry the older woman's fingers from the bridle.

"He's a breathin' still. And I'm a needin' a horse. Help me, please," she said.

Rhea looked at the soldiers, searched their faces as far as she could see. Then she ran her hand down the horse's neck and onto its left shoulder. The shoulder was caked and wet, the sticky wetness of blood. Rhea could feel the wound beneath her fingers. She examined the horse, its back, its legs, the other side. Except for the wound, it was sound enough. But it was done in, consumed by the war, the men and the whip they'd used.

Rhea felt in her pocket. The little cloth sack was there from the morning, Claudia's sack of sugar, the last vestige of tea and coffee and civilization. Twenty dollars a pound for sugar when it could be found, and Claudia had forgotten to put it in the sack when they fled. Rhea poured some of the precious contents into her palm and rubbed it against the horse's velvet lips. She stroked it and talked softly to the animal, rubbing the sugar between the mare's lips. Her great tongue and teeth eagerly sought Rhea's palm as she carefully bent her thumb and fingers back and away to dish up the flat palm and sugar.

"Good old girl," Rhea said. "You've been somebody's darling. Good girl.

Rhea offered one more palm of the sugar, then caught the bridle, and led Mrs. Singpiel and the horse along the flat land beside the road. They walked a long time—two women

32

and a limping horse among a retreating army
—unnoticed. Finally a cavalry lieutenant rode
across their path.

"You ladies can't go any further. A
precaution," he said from his high seat on the
horse. "You might warn the Yankees of our
withdrawal."

"I don't care nothing for your withdrawal or
your cussed war!" Mrs. Singpiel shouted. "I'm
going to fetch my dead. My man and boy's dead
with the conscripts. I care not a damn who wins
this war, boy. My cause is lost. Let me pass."
The look in her watery blue eyes and her trembling anger made the lieutenant ride on,
chancing any warning she might carry to fate.

Rhea looked at the woman. Tears ran down
her dumpling cheeks. Rhea remembered Mrs.
Singpiel's fried chicken and four-layered choc-
olate cakes at the church suppers. She remembered Lem Singpiel and his tall, lanky
fourteen-year-old son, Charlie, pressed and
formal in their Sunday suits as they took collec-
tion. "They may not be dead, Aggie," Rhea
said. "Don't give up hope till we see for sure."

"I give up hope 'fore daylight yesterday
morning when them *seces* come and woke us
up and dragged off my men to fight in a army

33

they hate. Lem's a Union man, straight. Even the state's right business couldn't make him fergit the Union. He didn't go off, like your man to join the Union boys, 'cause he thought I needed him to help with the little children at home. But the *seces* come and took him. He's dead and the boy, too. They'd die before they'd fire on the flag."

Rhea tightened her hold on the bridle. Like Lem and Charlie Singpiel and Andy Potts, her brother had strong Union views. Like them he'd voted against secession in choosing delegates to the Arkansas convention. The yeoman farmers of the northern counties had held firm for union. Independent men, they didn't want to be pushed into secession by the planters and the Johnson faction.

However, for some, the proud independence was their downfall. Lincoln's call for troops to force South Carolina back into the Union violated their strong conception of a state's right to govern itself and their pledge to uphold that right. Even then, even in that deadly April of 1861, four of their delegates had held out for union. But the convention and its chairman, Union man, David Walker, called for a unanimous vote to secede. Three votes changed under the pressure of circumstance and men's eyes. Only Isaac Murphy came home as he went away—an unconditional Union man.

Still, a lot of Arkansas men refused to join the state troops of the Confederacy—men like Lem, Charlie, Andy, and Joseph. They'd stayed on their farms, drawing their battle lines there against all comers. But Tom Hindman rousted them out, rounded them up out of their fields or beds, out of stores where they bought supplies, out of boarding houses and hotels. No place was safe; no excuse or conviction valid. Confederate soldiers by conscription, they marched under guard to battle. They were thrown into battle against one army by another army willing to sacrifice them, willing to gamble they would fight rather than be killed by the Union they professed to love. And so their rights were taken by the very men who had held such rights so dear.

Rhea began to see the wounded, walking on their own or carried along by friends, stringing out in the rear behind the artillery and troops. She and Mrs. Singpiel sought their men anew among them. Men reached up, asked for water, and went on uncomforted. Silent tears ran down Rhea's cheeks as she held their hands and

35

looked for Joseph. Once Rhea gave the horse's reins to Aggie and climbed into a wagon bed to turn a man whose back and shoulders suggested Joseph's form. But it was not Joseph. The soldier's place could have gone to someone else for he was dead.

Rhea watched closely now for her father. Since he was a doctor, he would be with the wounded. Just yesterday morning the rebels had come for him at his home infirmary. Rhea had been there, in town for church. Dr. Isaacs had sent her to take Claudia and Joey from Joseph's farm on the Van Buren Road to the safety of Lord's Vineyard.

Dr. Isaacs was not among the retreating Confederate soldiers, but Rhea found him at the Presbyterian church where the Confederates had a hospital. In the first light of Monday morning, she could see the limp green flag indicating the hospital. Her father was on the steps, supervising evacuation of some of the wounded. Dr. Isaacs was a stocky man. He looked older than his daughter remembered. The long day and night of fighting seemed to cast a grey shadow over his skin. His sleeves were rolled above his elbows. The apron he wore was dirty with the blood and debris of the soldiers.

"Papa," Rhea said. "Have you seen Joseph?"

Dr. Isaacs took a moment to shed the deadly nightmare of war and recover the reality of his daughter and his son. "I heard he fell at the peach orchard north of the river, but I've not seen him. No one brought him in yesterday or last night. Are Claudia and the boy safe?" Rhea nodded. "Was there any trouble getting to Vineyard?"

"It was a long cold walk, but nobody bothered us. The soldiers robbed Joe's house sometime after we left but we took some things with us before they came." Rhea remembered Aggie. "What about the Singpiels, Lem and Charlie?"

"I haven't seen them," her father said shortly. An orderly asked him something. He started back into the church. "Look at the orchard—that's where the conscripts were. Rhea, bury him here at the church. You'll have to bring Claudia and the baby to town for the funeral." He was gone then.

Rhea and Aggie walked on across the fields of bodies where stretcher-bearers still gathered the wounded. Burial details carried bodies unceromoniously and stacked them in piles on the field. Women are not used to battlefields.

37

Their eyes, their primal blood, are not accustomed to such things. But Rhea saw it clearly, the splintered trees and cratered earth. She looked east back toward the Borden place and saw the long hill climbing the ridge littered with men, flowers of the field, cut at random and abandoned. Soldiers stacked rails around a body, colorless against his gray uniform and golden epaulets. The orchard was ahead—trees blasted and uprooted, men crumpled so close together Rhea could barely walk between them. Mrs. Singpiel was gone, taking the horse with her in her search for her men. Rhea stumbled among the dead.

She could not remember now how Joseph looked. "Was he a boy? No," she thought. "Joseph is a man with a wife and son of his own." But the picture of the boy Joseph remained in her mind. "Was he wearing the coat Mama bought him in St. Louis? Rhea," her mind said, "Mama's been gone ten years. Joe was eleven when she gave him that coat." Still Rhea could not remember Joseph as a man in a war. She kept seeing the irresponsible boy who ran off when their father needed his instruments cleaned or a wound dressing replaced on a patient. The Joseph she sought was a tow-headed child with no place among these grizzled corpses.

Rhea bumped against someone. Reverie faded to reality. Other women searched among the bodies like she did. She knew them all. "I believe I seen your brother over that away," one of them said. And Rhea went in the direction the woman pointed.

Joseph Isaacs, Union man, lay on his stomach among four other soldiers. One arm stretched over his head; the other rested by his cheek. He looked like a sleeper, except there was a blanket of heavy frost over him. Rhea knelt beside him. The ground around him and the other dead soldiers was punctuated with fragments of paper cartridge and minie balls. Rhea touched one of the shining inch-long lead projectiles. The conical bullet was hollow at its base, to explode and engaged its three grooves in the rifled barrel, giving it more accuracy and power as it sped toward its target. The ground around her brother was littered with the metal.

"They only fired their powder," a voice said, and Rhea looked up at a man's figure silhouetted against the morning sun. "They charged and took Blunt's charge with blank guns. Them conscripts sure were not cowards, ma'am." The soldier walked on, carrying his gun by the barrel over his bony shoulder.

"No cowards," Rhea said softly. She stroked Joseph's cheek. His sleeper's eyes did not flutter open. She touched the coat that Mama had not bought him. "But so dead, so very dead." She looked at his long legs sprawled like a sleeper's. "Where are your boots, Joseph?" she asked and looked at the men near him. All had been systematically stripped of boots and anything else of value. Their pockets were turned inside out. A plug of tobacco too soiled with blood to chew was all that remained. "Damn thieves. Kill a man, then rob him." Rhea tried to turn her brother, but his body did not move. She tried harder.

"Let me help, child," a short, squat old man in rags said. Rhea did not know the man. His accent was strange to her ears. "He's froze to the ground. Their blood freezes them to the ground. I been chopping men loose all night. It's the onliest way to get them up." Rhea looked at his boots. The axe head rested by his foot. She saw the axe go up.

"No!" she cried. "Don't. Don't hurt him."

"He's dead, child. I ain't going to hurt him now."

"I mean, don't cut him," Rhea said.

The soldier lowered the axe. "Where's the wound?"

"I don't know," said Rhea looking the body over. "It must be underneath him."

"Damn," the old soldier said. "Hey, Bill," he called to his partner. "We're going to have to pry this one up. He's froze underneath. You wait over there, girl." The two men grunted and heaved. Bill used the axe as a pry bar until Joseph's body was free of the ground. They rolled it onto a blanket stretcher. The short man took the Sharps rifle Joseph had fallen on. Blocking Rhea's view with his shoulder, Bill took the watch from Joseph's waist pocket. They laid the axe and rifle on the body. Each man took an end of the blanket and started up the hill. Rhea looked at the place where Joseph had been. She bent swiftly and scooped up the bright minie balls with her hand and thrust them into her pocket.

"Where are you going?" Rhea asked.

"We'll carry him up to be buried for you," the old one said.

"He's not to be buried here," said Rhea.

"Once he's up on the ridge maybe you can get a way to take him off," Bill said.

Rhea walked the steep hill beside Joseph. She was lost in her own thoughts, thoughts of her shattered family, the shattered community, thoughts of her own husband somewhere beyond the Mississippi risking his life on fields like this. The two soldiers forgot her and talked merrily.

"Cold as it is," the old man said, "I believe it's better duty than when it's hot. Once I buried bodies in July. The fourth day, we'd just dig a hole right next to the body and roll it in with a pole 'cause when it hit bottom it'd explode. We couldn't hardly stand the stink. I'll always remember the stink of this war. Yes, sir, I will."

"I remember one time it started rainin' after we buried a batch. There we stood under a tree cussin' the water washing the bodies out. The worms all washed out on top of the ground, too, jest covering it as far as you could see. We had to skim 'em off the drinking water that shavetail lieutenant had made us bury in barrels. Times was tough then," Bill added.

"They were purty tough up there by the Borden house," his companion said. "Them boys that burned in the outbuildings got et by the damned hogs. Never thought I'd see hogs eatin' roast people. Damn!''

They walked on in silence. At the top of the ridge, the men started to set Joseph's body down alongside the pile of bodies already carried there.

"Wait," Rhea said. "My father's office is just over that way. If you'll carry my brother home, we can pay you."

"Lead the way, ma'am," Bill said.

The trio walked across the long desolate table of the prairie that gave the town and the battle of Prairie Grove its name. The house was more than a mile from where Joseph had fallen. They passed the gravediggers working on the shallow graves, passed the weeping women sitting beside their men. They passed the stacked bodies and the stacked arms.

"I'll take that gun," a corporal said, reaching for the Sharps rifle on Joseph's chest.

Rhea beat him to it and pulled it away by the butt. Her other hand slid onto the stock and her fingers closed over the trigger. "You may try," she said.

"Let her be," Bill said. They went on to the house.

They laid Joseph on the table in Dr. Isaacs'

office. Rhea gave each man a coin from her purse. Bill looked at the purse hungrily. "Guess we could take it all, ma'am, if we was thieves. Guess we could."

"We ain't thieves," the old man said. "Let's go back."

"Bill," Rhea said. "Since you aren't thieves, leave my brother's watch. His son will want it someday." She raised the rifle slightly.

"How'd you know that rifle's loaded?" Bill asked.

"God bless," said the old man. "She'll blow your damn head off, and she ought to. Let's get out of here. We're wasting time we could be workin' the field without no sass."

Bill muttered a profanity, handed over the watch, then followed the older soldier. Rhea could hear them fighting as they walked away. She checked the rifle. It was empty. But the pistol in her skirt was not if Bill came back.

Now Rhea looked about the little infirmary. She sat down, not wanting to begin the grim work before her. She bent forward studying the scuffed toes of her boots. Her mind held no thought, but wandered aimlessly about the past. The present compulsion to deal with the dismal circumstances intruded again and again, but she let action slip away as she sat looking blindly at her brother's dead body, at the room, at her own hands turning the wedding ring. Rhea did not hear the door open, did not turn to see the girl, Jane Wilson, enter. Tears streaked Jane's cheeks. She struggled for breath.

"Mrs. Dameron," Jane said, taking a breath. "Mrs. Dameron, they said you was here. Thank the Lord. I run all the way here. It's Ma, Mrs. Dameron, she won't quit her loom. Mrs. Dameron?"

Realizing that Rhea wasn't listening, the girl knelt before her, placing her hands on Rhea's knees. The girl's pale face, whiter than the tow hair that surrounded it, took shape slowly before Rhea's eyes. She blinked, stretched out her arm to take the girl's hand. "What did you say, Jane?"

"It's Ma, Mrs. Dameron. She won't leave her loom, but all the wool's wove up. She's weaving only the air."

"Your mother?" Rhea questioned. Mrs. Laura Wilson was the bulwark of the community, whose example held many a young wife straight. Her good sense shone out of her fine wide eyes and rose in soft counsel with her voice.

45

"Yes, ma'am, my ma," the girl said.

Rhea stood up. She opened the door and with Jane crossed back across the battlefield to the south and east. They stepped over bodies twisted into grotesque death statues. The sight of severed limbs and gaping wounds, no longer horrified their sensibility. They did not avert their eyes any longer. Somehow it seemed natural here that each body should be more ghastly than the last. This was a special world with its own reality, a reality apart from beauty and love. They walked silently, engrossed in the scene.

To climb the hill to the house, they had yet to cross a field stone wall. Jane scrambled over and ran ahead toward the shelled and pocked farmhouse. Rhea lifted herself onto the stones. Sitting she turned her legs and long skirt over the wall. Blindly she dropped to the other side. As she landed, she fell among the dead soldiers who had held up the wall. "I'm sorry," she said to the young man sitting back against the stones. "I didn't see you." The soldier did not answer but continued to stare off down the hill.

Rhea looked at his face, calm and young and beautiful with strong even features. His soft hair flipped in the wind. His gun lay across his lap, one hand on the barrel. The other hand rested across his body, fingers spread over the bloody wound that exposed his bowels. "My God," she said, stumbling away to her knees and hands, wretching the contents of her stomach on the ground beside the wall, then heaving emptiness in quick involuntary contractions. It was not death or its ugliness that sickened her, but the beauty of the dead boy, the sudden awareness of loss, the human thing he was and could no longer become—the mother's child, the beau, the husband, the farmer, the old man with a grandchild holding his hand. She saw it all, saw it die before her, the sense of what was normal, what a man had a right to expect. Rhea sat back on her heels, resting, wiping her eyes. She looked up at the farmhouse on the crest of the hill.

Further along the ridge two houses burned, torched by Union soldiers in retribution for the Confederate snipers they'd held. A couple of horse soldiers galloped across the long hill shouting, occasionally firing their pistols as other men carried fence rails and stacked them around the growing piles of bodies. Rhea saw Jane waving her to come on. She stood, brushed her skirt absently and started past the beautiful

47

dead boy up the hill. From the pile of bodies beside him, a hand caught her ankle, freezing the blood in her and causing her to cry out.

"Help me, ma'am. Don't let them hogs get me," a soldier buried among other bodies said. Rhea knelt, pulling away the dead men from the living. The wounded man reached out, and Rhea caught his hand. "For God's sake, keep them hogs off me."

"There aren't any hogs around here, soldier," Rhea said.

"There will be. Them rail pens they're buildin' is keepin' 'em off the dead piles, but they're hungry enough to keep comin' for the meat."

"Rest now," Rhea said, looking beyond the man's haggard face at the soldiers stacking rails around the dead. She saw no hogs. The animals by custom ran free to forage the woody hills until killing time. They became wild and wary and vicious. Hunters and farmers feared them for their cunning. And there was one more thing—with their weight and size they could strike a man low and hard, cut him down and go in for the kill with blinding speed. George Woods, a farmer along Cove Creek, had learned that. Woods carried off dead animals in the area as a service, and his hogs got used to tearing the dead carcasses of cows and horses. But one day, the farmer himself fell and the hogs devoured him. He was brought to Doctor Isaacs. Rhea had seen what was left of the body, and she winced, remembering.

"Water. Water, please," the soldier said.

Rhea looked about for a canteen. She found the dead boy's hung across his shoulder and chest. She fumbled with the buckle, trying not to look at the boy. Finally freeing the canteen, she brought it to the man. He drank greedily, water running down the sides of his mouth and onto his shirt front. Rhea had pulled back now, away from her feelings. A wall had gone up. She studied the wounded man, noting his color, weakness, breathing, looking at the left arm hanging limply in his sleeve. "Are you hurt anywhere besides your arm?"

"No, ma'am. I believe I am sound otherwise," the soldier said.

"Have you a knife?" she asked.

The soldier pulled a bowie knife from his boot, and Rhea split the sleeve away from his arm. She was careful not to move the limb roughly. She studied the wound and looked up into the man's face. It had gone white, his eyes fixed on something behind Rhea. She heard the

49

soft grunts and spun to see six hogs rooting among the dead. Rhea looked at the old black sow who led the herd, searching for the sow's tiny eye. The small orange orb set low in the fleshy cheek studied Rhea, cautious of this living one among the dead. A shoat moved closer to Rhea and she plunged the bowie knife into his shoulder.

Then the hogs were upon them. Rhea grabbed a broken Enfield by the barrel and swung it hard against the sow's snout. She squealed and ran back. Rhea came suddenly to her feet, still swinging the rifle with both hands and creating a space between her, the soldier, and the hogs. Then the pocket pistol was in her hand, banging bullets into the foreheads of the attacking hogs as Rhea turned in their midst. The black sow saw an opening and charged in, ripping Rhea's skirt with the long tushes but unable to hit the woman's legs with full force because of the deceptive skirt. She threw her head sideways, ripping the soft leather of Rhea's bootleg. Struggling to keep her feet, Rhea pushed the revolver down against the sow's head and fired. The black sow fell instantly. The gun clicked on an empty chamber. Rhea reached for a dead soldier's pistol. But the fight was over. Three hogs lay dead and the others had scattered down the hill.

"Nice shootin', lady," the Union cavalryman who had ridden up said.

"Why aren't you killing those damned hogs?" Rhea almost shouted.

"Easy, ma'am. They're private property," he said.

"That simple fact has not kept you from burning people's houses," she said.

"Those were Confederate sympathizers' places, I reckon we could consider those were Confederate hogs for attacking this Union corporal," he said and rode on with a companion, rollicking in the prospect of hunting hogs from horseback.

Rhea watched them ride off. She pulled the torn skirt aside to examine the torn boot and her leg. Finally she turned to the wounded man. "You're lucky," she said. "The bullet passed through your arm without hitting the bone. Can you stand up?"

The soldier struggled to rise, and Rhea helped him. Leaning on her, he stood shakily. Jane ran back to them. The trio walked slowly toward the farmhouse. As they walked, Rhea realized this was the worst of it—the worst fighting had been here around the house and outbuildings. Bodies were thick on the ground. At least some of the fighting had been hand-to-hand. Kansas had met Missouri at this plain white house. The bitterness and hatred that festered had spilled out, polluting the land. Rhea's skirt dragged across the dead as she stepped over them, holding the soldier. He looked around the littered yard. "It were a helluva fight, ma'am, helluva fight."

Jane's sister and sister-in-law ran from the back door to Rhea and Jane. "Is he one of ours?" the sister asked.

"It don't matter much now," the other said, taking Rhea's place. "I'll take him, Rhea. You see about Laura."

"Wash his arm with lye soap if you have it, and wrap it in something clean," Rhea said. She went with Jane then to the house. The porch of the building held more bodies, lifeless, spent in a struggle that here boiled down to nothing but hate and revenge for the bitter border years. There were no Kansas abolitionists now, no Missouri slaveholders. There were only dead men—men who had died hard.

Inside the women walked through the house, past the children huddled about an older girl, past the bullet holes that riddled the door frame. The main room contained a loom and spinning wheel, a large stone fireplace, a rope bed, a couple of chairs and a little table. There was a stairway leading to the main sleeping rooms upstairs. A trapdoor opened beneath it to the root cellar.

"We stayed down there," Jane said. "It was dark and cold. We could hear the shooting and killing. The children cried till there wasn't anything left to cry. Ma went up to get blankets and quilts. We was all scared, bullets whizzing around, but she climbed upstairs and got the cover. She threw it down to us. We could tell she was walking around from window to window. Pretty soon we hear the loom. I yelled out for her to come down to safety, but she wouldn't."

Laura Wilson still sat at the loom, weaving an unseen fabric and singing softly. "Jane," Rhea said, "bring me your pa's whiskey. Then build a fire and bring the children in to sit by it. Put on some water to boil for tea and cook whatever you have." Rhea went to Laura and sat down beside her. She said nothing, but watched Mrs. Wilson's hands moving expertly over the big loom just as if she worked her

53

finest wool. Rhea sat beside her a long time, watching her work, noting the bullet hole in the loom frame.

"We'll have to use wild dyes," Laura Wilson said. "But we can get a pretty red out of the pokeberries, like my ma used to. The secret's the mordant. We can make it bright and fast as before the war. I've studied on it. I've saved up horseshoes and old nails and bits of iron. Put 'em in the water. Add a mite of vinegar. Janey's dress will be pretty as storebought. It will."

Rhea reached out, placing her hand over Laura Wilson's on the loom. "Laura, let's quit awhile and have some tea. Some nice hot tea," she said. "I'm tired out, Laura. Let's get a bite and rest up."

Mrs. Wilson looked at Rhea, not really focusing on her, but trusting her. She stood up, catching the loom frame. Rhea helped her to the rocker by the flat hearth. The fire was going strong. Five red-eyed children huddled near it still under their quilts and blankets. Jane dropped the Dutch oven lid and it rang out. The children jumped together again but did not cry. Rhea took an extra blanket and tucked it over Mrs. Wilson's legs.

"That's a good fire, Jane," she said, as she

picked up the whiskey jug and poured it into a cup. Rhea looked at the food Jane was cooking, cornmeal boiling in water for a thick mush. Honey for sweetener. A nearly empty tin of tea. Rhea dumped the tea in a pot, poured boiling water over it, allowing it to steep in the crockery vessel as she went to check on the wounded soldier. The women had cleaned and bandaged his arm. They stood at the window watching him walk off leaning against another soldier.

"He saw someone he knew. Said he had to get back to his outfit," one of them said. "Sure does look feeble to be walking about, though." Rhea watched him, too.

"We did what we could. Maybe he'll get to a hospital. Let's go in by the fire," Rhea said, and they followed her.

She poured tea into the cup of whiskey and added the thick golden honey, stirring it into the steamy brew. She helped Laura Wilson with it as the other women filled their cups with the tea. They drank slowly and in silence for a time.

"When did you all come here with the children?" Rhea asked Jane's sister.

"Yesterday 'fore daylight. When we heard

the first shots," she said. "We gathered up the youngins and came over here."

"With our men gone," the sister-in-law said, sharing her tea with a child, "we couldn't think of anything to do but get to Laura's house. As it turned out our places were safer."

Rhea remembered yesterday before daylight. The shooting had awakened her, too. She had gone to the infirmary and found her father leaving with soldiers to help set up a hospital. Go get Claudia he had said. Rhea spent the balance of the day getting Claudia and Joey and moving her and the child to the Dameron home at Lord's Vineyard. These women and children had been in the midst of the battle.

"I think the fighting is finished," Rhea said. "Hindman's gone, and the Federals are in charge. They are cleaning up now—burying the dead, tending the wounded. You might as well stay here and rest up. There's no hurry now. Build up the fire in the other room. Make up the beds. Feed the children and put them down to rest. Laura needs to sleep. The whiskey tea will help. It won't hurt any of you. Stay warm, eat, and rest. That's the best to do for now. Later you can check your places. If they're like my brother's place, there's no hurry. I'll look

56

back in on Laura later today if I can. See your ma gets plenty of this tea, Jane."

"Rhea, don't come back. I ain't so bad as some," Laura Wilson's soft voice said. "I got my folks about me. I ain't so bad. Guess I was just put off by the noise and the killing. It was the screamin', the terrible screamin' and the faces of the dyin' ones and the killin' ones. I saw it so plain through my window in my own yard. Like I was at a stage play except it was real, and it couldn't be stopped till it ran its course."

Rhea was quiet thinking about what Laura Wilson said. "You must rest up today, Laura," she said at last. "No excuses. Jane, you see she stays in that chair or a bed till morning."

"Rhea, your family? Are they doing well?" asked Laura.

"My brother was killed, but my father and Claudia and the baby are safe."

"Joseph's dead? Don't seem real. He and my middle boy are the same age," Laura Wilson said.

"Nothing seems real right now," Rhea said. "Maybe we ought to thank God for that."

Jane walked to the back door with Rhea. As

she opened it, Rhea heard Laura talking to the women with her.

"Joseph Isaacs dead. Haven't you fed these children yet, girls? There's too much to do to sit here bawling and feeling sorry for ourselves. We're all together." Rhea smiled.

She made her way back across the ridge, dodging soldiers and bodies and a few wagons hauling the dead. A man looks at a battlefield and sees troop movements and deployments, the position of artillery and cavalry and infantry. But Rhea saw the debris that littered the field. Not the dead men and animals. Not the wrecked wagons and artillery. Not the dug up ground or uprooted trees. But the pages from a diary blowing across the winter fields. The daguerreotype carefully focused now decomposed, exposed to the elements and strangers' curious eyes. A pair of spectacles. All things that made the soldiers separate men— men with past and future, hopes and dreams, families. All lost in the indifference of this impersonal death by war.

They buried the dead in shallow trenches, Rebs together, Yanks together. But sometimes it was hard to tell, because Confederates took whatever they could find of boots and coats and guns, and because some of the Yanks were worn a little thin and also found their resupply on the field. And when after the war the bodies were moved slowly by wagon down the Fayetteville Road to final resting places in Confederate and Federal cemetaries, only young boys worried much about mistakes. Most grown men knew that, whichever side a soldier fought on, he was dead. Both belonged to another world, a forgotten time that held no reality—no widow's tears or poverty, no orphan's struggle, no pain of heart.

Sighing, Rhea climbed the infirmary steps, leaning heavily on the rail. The prospects of the house did not invite her. She wished her father or her husband were there. Someone to hold her. Someone. Something. Something beside the great sorrow.

"I'll not be needin' this here horse, Rhea." Rhea heard Mrs. Singpiel's voice from behind her. Mrs. Singpiel stood holding the wounded cavalry animal. "You might be able to doctor it up some, too. My men's going to be buried at the church so I won't be takin' 'em home, after all." Mrs. Singpiel walked away, leaving the horse tied to the porch banister.

Rhea went back into the infirmary and gathered a probe, other instruments, and rags from the bottom drawer of her father's cabinet. She saw that most of the medicine was gone—confiscated for the wounded. She heated a kettle of water in the kitchen and waited in the silent house, remembering dinner at the table with Papa and Mama and Joseph, a nice family, full of potential and hope. She walked to the bedroom off the kitchen where Joseph was born, where Mama died. There was a miniature of her on the dresser. Papa used the room for his patients, but it still retained Mama's touch in the curtains and samplers and plain furniture. The kettle whistled and Rhea returned to it, pouring some of the boiling water over the tray of instruments. The boiling idea was Mama's. It was a ceremony of cleanliness and good womanly household management, not common medical practice.

Rhea glanced at the table where Joseph's body lay, grotesquely shaped beneath the sheet. She saw beyond it the razor strop hanging on the wall, tribute to the independent will of children and the firmness of parents. She saw below the strop the two cane fishing poles in the corner. Dr. Isaacs gave up beating responsibility into

Joseph a long time ago, finally accepting his son for the man he was. Today Rhea was glad.

In the barn, she worked on the horse for almost an hour. She retrieved the bullet, washed the wound, and poured iodine over the raw flesh. She locked the doors with a chain and padlock Dr. Isaacs kept hanging in the little carriage shed. Since yesterday, her riding horse and Isaacs' buggy horse had both disappeared from the unlocked barn. This horse would not.

Returning to the house, she found Dr. Isaacs and Jesse Branch working over Joseph. Branch was the undertaker, a surly fellow who had no sympathy for anyone. Rhea dreaded facing him. Avoiding the table with her eyes, she went into the kitchen and began to clean her tools. Dr. Isaacs came in and sat down. He watched Rhea. She had inner strength. She had absorbed his lessons, accepted her responsibility. He was proud of her. Then he realized his daughter was a beautiful woman, too, with her fair hair, pale eyes, and smooth skin. She was erect and moved with grace and ease. Yet the realization of that beauty irritated him. Because, in the reality of that time, only he would ever know that not only was she a beautiful woman but also a first-rate doctor.

"There's to be a general service tomorrow afternoon," Isaacs said. "You can get Claudia here by then if you leave soon."

Rhea set her work aside. "You know, Papa, for a long time this morning I couldn't remember how old Joseph was. I kept thinking he was a little boy and Mama was alive."

"It was happier times then," her father said. "We were all together. I keep thinking how I ragged Joe for so many little silly things." He sat silently for a moment looking at his hands. "I'm sorry I let you go alone, Rhea. It was too hard. But the living always take precedence over the dead, even our own dead. Do you understand, Rhea?"

She nodded. A small tremor ran through her lower lip. "I understand," she said softly. "But I wish I didn't, wish I didn't have to. I don't like being brave, Papa."

Dr. Isaacs put his arms around his daughter and held her. "Somebody has to be brave— that's a rule as old as mankind and as new as each generation. It's your burden to carry and your glory, Rhea. Go on out now and get Claudia."

Rhea rode and walked the cavalry horse to Vineyard. It was late afternoon, too late to start

62

back, when she arrived. She ate her supper and fell asleep on the sofa, exhausted, listening to Claudia's violent crying. In the morning Hillary, the black woman, got their breakfast while Rhea hitched the buggy horse and saddled a riding horse. Just after sunup, the three women and the baby Joey set off for town.

Rhea looked for Dr. Isacs at the church, but could not find him in the crowd. She got Claudia a seat near Joseph's pine coffin and left Hillary with her. Claudia accepted the condolences, enjoying her grief thoroughly. It was easy for Rhea to slip away to find her father. He was in the infirmary, stuffing lint and bandages into a saddle-bag. Blackie Foard leaned against the table, a huge horse pistol protruding from his filthy plaid coat. If there was a general impression of Foard, it was of pervasive dirt. He was a small man covered from head to foot in dirt and grease and matted hair. There were two horses outside, but Rhea saw no other rider. Dr. Isaacs looked up as she entered. But he said nothing and returned to his work. Rhea looked at Foard. Their eyes met—a clash of icy blue. Foard looked off. Something was wrong. She wasn't supposed to be here. She started to speak.

"There's a clean sheet in the bedroom cupboard. Get it," Dr. Isaacs said abruptly as she opened her mouth.

Rhea went into the bedroom and got the sheet. Her father came to the door behind her. "Don't rip it up," he said loudly. "I'll roll it myself later." Then he spoke to her softly, "Foard has some wounded men hidden in a cave. I'm going with him. I'll need your help later probably. When I can, I'll send word."

"You're takin' too long," Foard said. "Let's get."

Rhea watched her father mount the extra horse. He looked at her over the saddle as he stepped up. Foard let him ride off in front. He did not look back.

She returned to the funeral and slipped quietly through the crowd to sit beside Claudia. Rhea looked at the row of caskets. There were so many. Fresh pine boxes sat in a neat row across the front of the church. Town people, Federal soldiers, families sat there together, shocked and rigidly polite under the burden of countless deaths.

Aggie Singpiel leaned forward across the pew back, putting her hand on Rhea's shoulder.

"The Yankees hung Noel Canup and Jed Buchannan at Cane Hill yesterday."

"Why?" Rhea said, turning to her. "They're harmless old men."

"Harmless or no. Blunt made examples out of them for all the snipers poppin' at his men," Mrs. Singpiel said. Rhea turned back. She sighed, sick of war. "Wouldn't let them be buried either. Just left them hang all day. Last night three young girls cut them down and buried them." Aggie Singpiel sat back.

Rhea tried to listen to the sermon. Joey squirmed in Hillary's arms until she sat him on the floor. Rhea watched him crawl away clumsily. He sat up among the caskets, smiled stunningly his toothless grin, and patted the boxes with his soft baby hands. Rhea picked him up. Again she tried to listen, but she kept thinking about Blackie Foard and the big pistol he displayed. Rhea began to cry unnoticed among the mourners, alone in her memories and fears. She pressed her wet cheek against Joey's baby curls.

Outside town, men and soldiers lowered the caskets into graves and quickly shoveled the loose dirt on top. In a final burst of grief, Claudia threw herself on Joseph's grave and wept long and loud. Rhea knelt and touched her shoulder. She wept louder. Rhea stood then, waiting with the tears running unrestrained down her cheeks. Hillary bounced the baby softly on her hip. Finally Rhea led Claudia to the buggy for the slow ride back to the Vineyard.

4

AFTER midnight sometime, the door to Rhea's bedroom swung open. Rhea was not asleep. She saw Hillary plainly by the lamp she carried. "There's a man in the kitchen wants you. He says he has a message from Dr. Isaacs."

Blackie Foard waited for Rhea. She listened intently as he spoke. "Doc says he needs your help. You're to bring a saw and more bandages and a basin or two. Come on, I've got to get you there before sunup."

Rhea dressed quickly and met Foard at the barn. "Sure hope you can ride, Missus Dameron. It's a rough trip."

They rode across the winter landscape, heading away from the direction of town, across the valley and up the hill to the southwest. Town was dark except for the light at Doc Isaacs' house. In a little while, when Rhea looked back, it was dark, too. Flint rocks sparked when the iron shoes of the horses struck them right, and that was the only light for many miles. Foard rode his horse hard among the rocks and down the rough grades. Rhea could hear the animal's breathing and kept up with Foard, though she hated pushing her own horse blindly and mercilessly in the night.

"By God," she said not cussing, "I hope you don't ride us off a bluff."

"By God," Foard said, not cussing, "I won't."

That was the last either said until the first light began to color the sky. Finally they rode off a steep ridge and down into a creek bottom. "We're almost there," said Foard. "Get down and tie your horse up here."

Rhea obeyed and tied her mount to a persimmon tree. Foard waited for her, then led the way up the mountain through the rocks and brush. Rhea looked up the mountain. She saw nothing to indicate their destination. She turned her ankle on one of the fist-sized loose rocks. Foard heard her stumble.

"Reckon if rocks is ever worth anything Arkansas'll be the richest state," he said. "Right here we got more rocks per acre than a man can haul. One year I tried pilin' 'em up at my place thinking I'd have a good field next

68

spring and a good crop. Next spring I had a good crop—damn near twice as many rocks. I give up then and went to raisin' goats." Foard stopped abruptly and held back a cedar limb. "Duck down, ma'am. It's a might low."

Dr. Isaacs was waiting for Rhea. "Wash up," he said. "And come over here."

Rhea poured water in a basin by the fire and scrubbed her hands with the creamy lye soap. She dried them on a length of sheeting and wrapped the ends around her waist and tied them in back, making an apron over her riding skirt. She went to where her father knelt beside a soldier. The man's color was gone; his eyes sparkled with pain against the pallor. There was a bloody drainage on the bandage tied across the man's chest.

"Did you bring the saw?" Isaacs asked. Rhea nodded. "Give him wine sop and then dress the wound. When you're finished come to me. They all need tending," he added wearily. "We must rig a drip bandage on a man. I've got to take an arm off in a little while."

Rhea looked at her father. He had not slept in days, not since the battle. As he walked off, he staggered and caught himself against the wall. Rhea covered the soldier with the blanket

69

and went to her father. "Papa, I can feed the men and change their dressings by myself. Mr. Foard can help if I need it. You must sleep. You won't be worth anything pretty soon if you don't get some sleep."

Dr. Isaacs studied the five men lying along the wall. He blinked to clear his burning eyes. Rhea was right. She could handle things; he did need to sleep. "Watch the one at the end closely. They hurt him bringing him here. He lost a lot of blood."

All morning Rhea worked over the soldiers. She washed their faces and hands, fed them the strengthening bread dipped in wine. She boiled and scrubbed the bandages and hung them around the cave to dry. Foard carried and boiled water over the small fire. He made a kind of thin soup from what he found in the packs of the men. He helped Rhea lift the men. Once an owl hooted near the stream. Foard got up and stood in the tiny mouth of the cave for several minutes with his hand on the butt of the pistol. Finally he disappeared. When he came back, he carried a stack of quilts with a dozen potatoes, a ham shank, and a bag of coffee on top.

"Their folks brought it. Leave it down the

creek a ways so if they're followed they won't give away the cave," he said. Rhea took the quilts and covered the men better while Foard rigged a spit and hung the ham over the fire. He made coffee and called to Rhea, "Come have a cup of hot, Missus Dameron."

Rhea went to the fire and wrapped a rag around the burning tin cup, absorbing the warmth in her hands and smelling the brew. "Wonder where they got coffee?" she asked. "We've been boiling grain or okra for months."

"Never know what folks have hid back," Foard said. "I reckon even in hard times you could find treasure in these old hills."

Rhea picked up a potato. "Who'd have thought two years ago a potato would be a treasure? Mr. Foard I don't know why we're hiding these men."

"Why, Ma'am, they was with a bunch of conscripts. They brought 'em in from out west of Prairie Grove, out past Cincinnati. They fought pretty good with the officer holdin' his gun to their heads, but when he lit out toward the river to fight with Shelby and Marmaduke, they went off the other way. They was carrying a couple of wounded men, so they was movin' pretty slow. About nightfall the officer come

71

back and didn't find 'em alive or dead. So he and a bunch of partisans come a hellin' in after 'em. They caught 'em in a barn and shot 'em to pieces. Me and my brothers rode in as they was ridin' out. We'd been hunting in the Nations and missed the impressment. We got 'em up here, figurin' they weren't too popular with the Rebs or the Yanks. They're all my neighbors 'cept that one on the end. I don't know him. Don't have no papers. Guess they robbed him, too."

Rhea drank her coffee, looking at the unknown man. "He's in bad shape," she said. "The others are better; they'll make it. But . . . I don't know. What about his people—how'll they ever know where he is or what hapened to him?'

'They'll never know, ma'am. Lots a folks around this here country won't never know what become of their people. One of my brothers went out West to look for gold in '49. We ain't heard whether he's dead or alive in ten years. There's a lot of folks like us now."

Rhea rose, set down her coffee, and filled a cup with soup. She went to the unknown man. Wiped his face from a basin and lifted his head gently. His eyes opened. "Mary," he said. "Where's the kids?"

"They're fine. Drink this," she said and touched the cup to his lips. He swallowed the soup slowly.

"They're alone, Mary. I got to get home," the soldier said, fighting to rise.

"Easy, son, easy," Dr. Isaacs said, taking the man gently. "Rhea, there's morphine in my bag. Bring it." Once the injection penetrated his blood, the soldier lapsed into unconsciousness. "It's time to take the arm," the doctor said.

After the surgery, Rhea set up a canteen as a drip bottle over the freshly bandaged arm. A length of cloth from the bottle to the limb kept the bandage moist, preventing it from sticking to the raw wound. She joined Dr. Isaacs by the fire.

"Where did you get morphine?" she asked.

"The Yankees have plenty and are generous enough when they are not looking," he said. "Rhea, we need more lint, more medicine, more everything. You'll have to go to Vineyard. Can you find your way home and back by morning?"

Rhea nodded.

73

"I'll take her out," said Foard, "see if I can't rustle up some cedar boughs or something for bedding."

Rhea bundled up and stepped to the door. She looked back over the dim interior. Her father was already working over one of the men, and did not notice when she left.

Foard led Rhea down the creek and gave her directions. "Missus Dameron," he said, "it's a long ride to your place. I can come if you want."

"No," Rhea said. "The doctor will need you more. My family will be at Vineyard by now. They'll have a good supper waiting. I'll sleep a couple of hours and be back by morning." She spurred off, already going over the list of things she'd need.

The back door was open, and she went inside. No one was in the kitchen, so Rhea hung up her coat and called out, "Anybody home?"

Both Hillary and Claudia came through the inner door. "Where have you been?" Hillary asked. "You look wrung out."

"I am wrung out. Is there anything to eat?" Rhea asked.

74

Hillary filled a plate, and Rhea ate slowly, methodically.

"Where were you?" Claudia asked.

"Father's with a family down with fever. I was with him," Rhea answered. "He sent me to rest and pick up a few things."

"There's nothing here we can spare," Claudia said. "We need everything for ourselves. I hope you didn't bring the sickness home."

"We'll see, Claudia, we'll see," Rhea said. She added nothing more but ate steadily until the plate was clean. Then she stood up slowly. "I have to leave in a few hours, so I'll say good night and see you both sometime tomorrow."

She went through the kitchen door down the papered hall and up the stairs to her bedroom. Rhea fell onto the sofa before the fire. She shoved the toe of one boot against the heel of the other and peeled the boot off. She tried the second boot, but it did not give. She bent and pulled, falling forward on the sofa when the boot came off. For awhile she lay that way, still holding the boot. "Get up," she said aloud at last. "You've got to get up." She got up finally, undoing her skirt and shirt as she crossed the room. "Move, cat," she said to the feline snug on the Drunkard's Path quilt. She went

immediately to sleep. Later Hillary covered her
and picked up the discarded clothing and boots.
She laid fresh clothes on the sofa, tended the
fire, and went off to her own room.

By breaking daylight Rhea was on the ridge
above the creek bottom where Blackie Foard
had brought her yesterday. Suddenly she heard
a dry flat *thwack* sound. She reined up, listened. Twice more she heard the sound. She
nudged the horse in tight against the trees and
waited. Two men emerged from the cave
laughing, carrying blankets over their
shoulders. A lantern swung merrily in their
midst. One man had each arm through a kettle
bail; the other ate greedily from the ham shank.
Rhea's heart pounded now, pushing against the
wall of her chest. Partisans had found the cave.
Three more men came out with a lantern, more
plunder boots, hats on top of their own hats.
Then two more appeared. The last two stopped
just outside the doorway. The young one lifted
his lantern over the path. The older man had
Dr. Isaacs' saddlebag over his shoulder. He
reloaded and replaced his Army Colt in its high
leather holster buckled over his jacket at the
waist. His black hat hid his face from Rhea.
He reached up suddenly with both hands and

removed the hat, stroked the heavy white hair into place, and reset the hat firmly. Rhea saw plainly the full white beard, the fiery rat-keen eyes as he lit a cigar. Crysop! Eleazar Crysop and his cherished son, Sweet William, stood talking as Rhea watched, hidden in the trees. Crysop slapped the boy on the back amiably, and they went down where the others held their horses. The guerrilla band rode off down the creek.

Rhea waited, numbed by the cold and fear of what she would find, until their sound no longer echoed through the dark valley. She climbed quickly to the cave. The cooking fire still burned, throwing eerie shadows over the walls. Rhea picked up a burning brand and went from body to body. A bullet had been placed expertly at the base of each skull behind the left ear. Her father lay facedown among his patients. They were all dead, executed. The unknown man must have died while she was gone, because a blanket was pulled over his face and he had not been shot. Rhea looked about her. Blackie Foard was not there. She turned to leave, but caught a movement out of the side of her eye. The unknown man's good arm came up and ripped the blanket from his face. She jumped.

"Missus," he said. "Help me, please." Rhea went to his side. "I'm dyin'." She took his hand. "I don't mind dyin', ma'am. I don't. It'll be kind of a relief. But my two children are alone. Their ma's dead. I'm gone. The doc saved me this long by pulling up the blanket when Crysop's gang come in. Anyways I been gone four days. There ain't nothin' left for my kids to eat." He clutched Rhea's hand hard. "Ma'am, I'm givin' my children to you. Ride west toward Cincinnati. Turn off along that baldy bluff on the south and ride along it till you come to a creek. From there go left about two mile. My place is settin' there on the other side. I'm givin' my children to you, ma'am. Take good care of 'em. God bless you," he said and closed his eyes. "It was Crysop hisself done all the shootin' in here. I swear that with my dyin' breath." Rhea sighed, placing his hand across his chest. She felt the carotid artery along his windpipe, then pulled the blanket up.

Rhea stood up, swallowing back a sob for them all—the soldiers, her father, the unknown man who stayed alive long enough to bequeath her his orphaned children. She cried, leaning against the wall in the cave of dead men. "It's not fair," she said, pounding the firebrand against the wall, kicking loose rocks, staggering in anger and pain as she lashed out. Then she stopped, standing erect and still by the fire. There was an apple on the floor, a bloodless red cider apple. She squatted beside the sole survivor of the carnage and plunder. She reached slowly for the pippin and grasped it powerfully. Then she went outside.

5

CHRISTMAS was less than three weeks away when Sarah and I came to live at Lord's Vineyard. Yet it was not a time of happy anticipation. In just a few days, we had lost our pa and buried him beside Rhea Dameron's father and her brother—all three, victims of a battle they had not wanted to fight. It was not a merry time for us or for anyone who lived in the mountains. It was a time of coffins. Even before the war we were always poor and hanging on till spring. But that winter of 1862, the poverty was severe. It was a poverty of hope as well as of material things. Since March we had been caught between two armies—Blunt's Army of the Frontier trying to establish firm control over the land they had won at Pea Ridge, and Hindman's Confederates trying to recruit a new army and push Blunt out. Most of our own men had been gone for a long time. Some with the Yanks. Some sent off East with the Confederates to fight in Virginia and Tennessee. Arkansas was essentially undefended in the north, an easy victim, and the partisan rangers knew that.

That summer, in the beginning, the Confederates authorized ranger groups to impress horses and supplies and men for the new army. But it was not long before the bands of ten or twelve raiders began to see the advantage to be gained by taking things that could be sold to defray their ever increasing expenses. Some of the canniest partisan leaders rode into Van Buren for their Confederate commissions, and then, rode the few hundred miles north to Springfield, Missouri, for their Union papers. In that way they were legal if stopped by either army. They could easily surrender any plunder, but ride away with their lives to make up for their loss. They were pure robbers, turning a profit at the expense of civilians of both sides. During the summer and fall they ravaged the towns and farms taking anything that was not hidden, torturing their victims till they revealed the hiding places. Most families had several hiding places so that some valuables remained even after a raid, but by December there was not much to hide. Life, a very meager life, was all that remained.

Yet even that poor life was threatened by a

81

savage who rode out of Kansas still waving a brightly burning torch for abolition. His name was Eleazar Crysop. Crysop was like most partisans in his thievery but worse because of his fanaticism. Crysop came to punish us—to burn and kill us for our taint of slavery or tolerance of it. The fact that there were less than fifteen hundred slaves in our entire county did not seem to bother him, nor did the fact that we were mostly a Union county. He saw only what he wanted to see, and he saw it with a steady and merciless eye. Like a patriarch from the Bible, he towered above other men, shaking his mane of white hair, stroking his snowy beard. For us he had chosen destruction and wrote, "Without the shedding of blood, there is no remission of sins."

More than any guerrilla Crysop instilled fear, for he came to terrorize and to kill. We all knew. He made that plain when he pulled Ned Elmer, an old farmer with two slaves, and his eleven-year-old grandson from their beds, hung them, and cut their hearts out in front of the Negroes and Mrs. Elmer. He locked her in the house and set fire to it. Folks said he sold the Negroes in Texas, but I do not know the

truth of that. *Crysop!* We all knew his name
and what it meant.

Even my sister Sarah who was just seven under-
stood the name. When I wanted privacy, I
could look around intently and say, "I hear
horses coming. Run, Sarah, run. It's Crysop."
She usually hid someplace, and I could escape
to other pursuits unencumbered by a baby-
sister. But lately, since coming to Vineyard,
Sarah did not always do the predictable.

There was, for example, the December afternoon the Crysop ploy backfired totally. I'd sent
Sarah off in terror and was making my way
along the shallow clear creek, turning over
rocks with a stick and looking for crawdads. I
heard the kitchen door slam and looked up to
see Rhea Dameron coming fast across the field
toward me. She wasn't wearing her hat or coat,
she was moving very fast. Sarah must have told
on me. I did something then that was not smart
—I ran. If I was fast, Rhea was faster. Halfway
up the hill she had my heel. I kicked, and she
had them both. Then I was going down the hill
on my back behind her. I figured she'd let me
up at the creek, but she didn't.

"Goddamn you," I said, cussing and kicking

and catching hold of anything I could get my hands on. "Crazy old woman trying to drown me. Damn it to hell, let me go!"

She didn't say anything but jerked me loose so hard my head banged the ground, and I swallowed the next two cuss words and nearly bit my tongue in two. At the barn she let go my feet and grabbed my hand. She pulled me through the door into the harness room and closed the door. I could see she was breathing hard and sweat stood on her forehead even in the cold. Overall, she was just as wet as me. She was about spent, but I'd learned a lesson coming down the hill. This time I didn't think I could outrun her. I reached for a dandy brush and raised it to throw.

"Boy," she said. "You've got enough to work out for this afternoon. Throw that brush and you'll be cleaning harness till you're ninety."

I drew the brush back higher, watching her face. She didn't blink or move. Since the funeral of Doctor Isaacs and my pa, she'd been serious and real quiet. I figured when she let go I didn't want to be on the other end of it. I sat the brush down and stepped behind a saddle rack.

84

"Don't hide from me," she said. "Come out of there and sit down of that keg."

"You goin' to hit me?" I asked.

"Do you need hitting?" I wasn't about to answer that. "Come out and sit down. I'll not hit you."

"Or whip me?" I said, bargaining.

"Don't push your luck, boy," she said. I came out and sat on the keg. She raised her hand to push her hair back. I ducked and fell off the keg squarely on my rear.

Suddenly she sat down on some grain sacks and was laughing, tears running down her cheeks. It was not like she was laughing at me, but at us both squared off in that tack room. And her laugh was so good, I laughed too.

"You know, boy, I said I wasn't going to hit you. I generally keep my word," Rhea said, wiping her eyes. Then she looked straight at me, not laughing anymore. "I don't like what you've been doing around here. You terrorize your sister. Sass Hillary. Make a hog wallow out of a decent bedroom. You use your grief and self-pity against those wanting to help you. And you always take the biggest piece of pie. Lately I've not been myself so you've been

85

getting away with it. But I'm back, boy. And we're going to have an understanding."

I didn't like this turn of events. My ma had been dead four years. I wasn't going to take anything off a woman. "You ain't my boss," I said.

"Who is your boss?" she asked.

I stammered a little, "Well, I reckon now I'm my own boss."

"Good," she said. "If you're old enough to be your own boss, you're old enough to listen to straight talk and take responsibility for your own action. Not one person in this household is your personal slave or fool. You are here because we want you, but you are taking advantage of your grief and your age. A gentleman doesn't take advantage, boy. He takes responsibility. Until you learn that and rein yourself in, you won't be a man if you're as old as God. Your responsibilities will not be unbearably great with us. But you will do chores. You will be respectful. And you will not exploit the credulity of one younger and less knowledgable than yourself. You will do these things . . ."

"Wait," I said. "What's cred, credulity?"

"That means you won't trick people who aren't as smart as you for your own advantage,"

86

Rhea said. "You'd better begin to have lessons every evening." I squirmed.

"I can read and write and cipher some. That's enough," I said.

"You've set a limit on yourself, have you?" she asked. I nodded. "I have not. You will do these things for your own good, boy, for the self-respect you'll need as a human being. Remember that. Remember I kept the wood box full and did the other chores a long time before you came. You are not doing me a favor. I can still do them better and faster. But you're doing your share. Now that's settled. It is settled?" she asked me.

"Yes, it's settled," I said.

"Good. Let's go get dry. I'm freezing."

We walked out the door together. Rhea put her hand on my shoulder like I was her boy. Just before we got to the house, she stopped me. "John Luke," she said. "Crysop is no joke. Anytime you mention his name I want to know you are telling the truth. If you say you see him coming, I have to know for sure." She looked at me, straight in my eyes. "It's important. I have to be able to count on you."

6

AFTER that day in the tack room, I thought about what Rhea said. I began to take hold. I kept things up pretty well, and nobody told me to do them. But women, and it was a household of women, were a burden to me sometimes. Joey Isaacs was the only other male, and he was still getting his pants changed.

Rhea knew my problem, I think, because she often took me with her when she visited her father's old patients. She let me stay around when people came to Vineyard. She gave me books and talked with me about medicine when I asked. My world began to open up as I watched her listening to those who came, as if there were no other voices calling her, as if there was no voice of her own inside her. When she listened, and they had finally talked out, she gave them herbs from her pantry, or cleaned a putrid wound on a filthy body, or fed their starving child from her meager table, or rode off from Vineyard with them to see one too ill to come or to take food where it was needed. I never heard her be unkind or cruel. She accepted them all as they were, healed and mended them, tried sometimes to teach them better ways for their own good, not hers. There was much sadness in her life and work, but she found peace in helping and taught me by example.

Medicine was sometimes hard to come by. On the Confederate market quinine sold for almost two hundred dollars an ounce, too much for a country healer or mountain people. It was even more expensive when bought from the black marketeers who profited from scarcity. It was a lucrative and common pastime, and the federals even condoned occasional smuggling in the South. Lincoln and Congress allowed the trade "when it seemed advantageous."

Generally, smuggling was advantageous to somebody. For a while an outfit called the Adams Express Company, for a two-dollar fee, would deliver quinine to any Confederate post office. The buyer ordererd and paid the drug company, and the shipment followed. But sometimes morphine was in the envelope instead. It was hard to tell it from quinine.

Dealing in drugs was hazardous in many

ways. Toward the end of the war, Rhea had almost given it up, substituting home grown remedies made from poppies or berries indigenous to our area. Dandelion could be substituted for calomel. Blackberry cordial could be used against dysentary. Like women throughout the South, she raised white poppies in her gardens for opium. The Confederacy supplied the seeds. One pharmacist in a drugstore drew a military exemption, and he helped with the growing, buying, and preparation instructions. Boiled into a paste, dogwood berries provided an alkaloid medicine comparable to true quinine made from cinchona bark. In late summer and fall, as malaria or ague swept over the populace, it provided some relief. Our miracle drug was whiskey. It was easy to come by in our hills. The women also made a number of fruit brandies with medicinal benefits.

The drug smugglers who came into our hills also brought another commodity, more precious to Rhea than the medicine—information. They brought news of new treatments, simple things today but new then, plaster of Paris for broken bones, bromine to use against gangrene and to protect doctors from infection. Spraying the air with bromine or sodium hypochloride made the environment purer, but abrasions on hands could also be painted with it to reduce staff danger of infection.

Rhea and I had been at Cane Hill all day looking in on many of Dr. Isaacs' former patients. They were mostly old people, who didn't trust strangers, especially city doctors. Without Rhea's calls they'd have reverted to yarb doctors and granny medicine. She listened to all their symptoms, cooked them a pot of beans or mush, made cornbread, cleaned their beds and bodies, found girls to cook and clean when she went away. It was an exhausting business. It was boring, too, as far as I could see.

I liked watching any medical procedures, but the nursing chores seemed better done by hired girls. No matter how Rhea explained the healing effect of care, I felt it a tedious task short on miracles, long on patience. And yet she was right, for I have seen a hopeless case heal with loving care while the same patient treated scientifically would weaken and die.

Still, I was a child, and Rhea had ways to keep me busy. She had me fetch wood and water and run errands. For an hour I'd been under foot. I rocked wildly before the fire until Rhea gave me a stern look over her shoulder and turned back to the bed.

"Mrs. Graymer," she said gently to the withered old woman, so pale and small beneath the quilt. "I'm going along now, but Esther's going to be here with you. You're to eat the good food she brings you—every spoonful. She's supposed to clean your place up every day so don't run her off. When you get up and about, you can take your meals with her and her ma. They're going to move in your little shed in return for the care, you remember? But they won't be in your house or underfoot. They agreed to that." Rhea smiled at Mrs. Graymer, who smiled a toothless smile back.

"Guess I can get used to it," Mrs. Graymer said. "Least I can do, the war making so many homeless."

"You're a generous woman," Rhea said. That was Rhea's way, helping people and letting them take the credit.

Rhea picked up her things, and we went outside. I skipped down the walk, free of sitting and quiet, free of the smell of old people, sickness, stale air, and chamber pots. Rhea drove us past the Cane Hill Academy and the little church. We stopped at the store, my reward for a long day. I diligently studied a sparse selection of stick candies. The war had ruined everything. I saw Rhea out of the corner of my eye talking with Ned Edgars, the pharmacist or at least our equivalent. Rhea always stopped and talked with Edgars. I figured she was discussing Mrs. Graymer's needs. I made my selection. Rhea paid. We returned to the buggy. I settled back for the long drive to Vineyard. This late it would be dark before we got home. Rhea settled the rugs over us and clicked to the horse. But instead of heading toward home, she turned the mare toward the mountains.

"Ain't we goin' home?" I asked. Normally I did not accompany Rhea late in the evening.

"I have a small emergency, John Luke. I'm afraid I'll have to take you with me this time."

"We'll miss supper," I said, tired of the day, the prospect of more sick people, and Ned Edgar's help. "What's the emergency?"

"We'll see," she said. "We'll see," was Rhea's best evasion, an iron door to questions.

"Female problems, I bet," I slumped back, sure of my diagnosis in the face of her silence.

We drove for a couple of hours, and I drifted off in the rhythmic swaying of the little buggy.

When I awoke it was pitch black, and the buggy was parked. Rhea was gone. I looked around for a cabin or something, but we were pulled up among trees and rocks. I yawned and pulled the blanket up high around my neck. I listened to the wind, felt a sting of sleet hit my cheek. The wind carried Rhea's voice and a man's from a stand of trees. Naturally I walked toward the sound. Through the trees I saw her and a man wearing a long overcoat and bowler hat. He sat on his heels on the gate of a little peddler's wagon. There was a small pile of goods on the ground in front of Rhea. The man was a stranger to me. I settled back, warned by that child's sense of adventure, against a tree to watch and listen.

"I need smallpox vaccine," Rhea said. "Enough for three or four people."

He turned to the wagon's interior and brought out the vaccine. "Some works; some don't," he said. "Seems like nasty stuff, being scraped off sores and all. M'am, I got something here you're sure to need. He pulled out a wooden chest, opened it, scrapped some corn aside, and tugged out a blanket-wrapped object. He unwrapped it carefully, revealing a cowhide pannier. "It's made by Dr. Squibb's company

94

for the army. Every regiment is issued one. There's fifty-two different medicines, each numbered for easy reference." He held a bottle in the flickering light for Rhea to see the number on the cork. "Besides that there's matches, candles, condensed milk, spatula, tourniquets, sponges, and oiled silk." The peddler continued to reveal the treasures.

"How much?"

"Five hundred Yankee," the peddler said.

"I heard the army pays about one hundred dollars each," Rhea said.

"You ain't the army," he said. "And the hand delivery's more difficult here."

"Sell me the sponges separate?" Rhea asked. In that hard time, we did not have sponges and were forced to use rags. As it turned out, that was fortunate because the boiled rags held fewer bacteria than the porous sponges. But we wanted sponges.

"Can't, m'am. She all goes together," he said.

"I guess I can spend my money better than for that pretty case," Rhea said, touching the case. "Have you chloroform?"

"Some," he said. "But you'll have to take some ether with it."

"I don't want ether. It blows up around a flame."

"Nobody else wants it either so I kind of extend my chloroform with it," the man said. "To get the one you have to take some of the other."

"Give me what you can," Rhea said, and he went inside. "You're sure that this Paris plaster works?" He nodded. "Add plaster to the water, never water to the plaster?"

"That's it, m'am. You got it down. They're using it in all the army hospitals now."

"Well, I'll pay up," Rhea said.

They figured the money, and Rhea handed over the gold and Yankee bills. "It's been most pleasant dealing with you, m'am. And just to show you my heart's on the right side, I'll throw in this bit of silk thread free." The smuggler closed his wagon then and drove off while Rhea began to move her supplies back to the buggy. When I saw her coming, I went back and pretended to be asleep.

"Is that you, Rhea?" I said, feigning drowsiness.

"Who were you expecting, John Luke?" she said, raising my feet and pulling a pair of men's trousers from the buggy. She leaned back against the wheel and pulled the pants on under her skirt. Pockets were sown all along the fronts and sides of each leg. She filled them carefully with her purchases and pulled her long skirt down over them at last. The rest she shoved under the seat except for the ether. "Don't mess with that," she said. "It'll blow your hand off, burn you up." I recoiled from it. "John Luke, if you ever see that man again, you don't know him. Understand?"

"How'd you know I saw anyone?"

"I didn't," she said. "When I left I covered you up with my blanket. Now it's next to you. You had to get up."

We started home then, each of us eager for the comforts of Vineyard in the coming storm. The mare trotted quickly down the mountainous road. We passed a mill, quiet and serene in the night, only one small light showing.

"I bet most folks are in bed asleep by now," I said. "Reckon they don't know what goes on this late at night or how pretty and strange things are with the moonlight and the storm blowing in."

"I reckon not. Flour gets ground in daylight. Stores get run in daylight. Fields get plowed in daylight. But people get sick at night. You know I sometimes fall asleep, but that little horse takes me home."

"She's a good horse," I said. "Ain't you scared you'll freeze to death if you fall asleep?"

"Are you cold?"

"Not real, no, m'am," I said.

"Sit closer and pull up the cover," Rhea said, and pulled my cap lower over my forehead. We rode on in silence for a while, listening to the wind and sleet hitting the back of the buggy.

"Still it's pretty and strange," I said. "Like in stories. I'm glad our Indians ain't mean no more."

"Me, too," Rhea said. "But your language is mean to my ears, boy. I thought we had worked out 'ain't' and double negatives."

"Oh," I said. "That's my informal way of speaking. I know better, but there's times when proper ain't right. Puts folks off."

"I see," she said. We drove on in silence then, the sleet getting stronger, the moonlight fading in and out among the clouds.

"I'm sure hungry," I said. "Be glad to see our turn."

Rhea reached under the seat and handed me a little box. "There's some cake in there from Elsie Barnes."

"She's the one with a sick baby this morning?" I asked. Rhea nodded and I ate the buttery pound cake. It melted away in my mouth. "It's good. Mrs. Barnes is a good cook," I said, offering Rhea a slice. We both ate in silence. I let my eyes close in pure pleasure, but suddenly they popped wide open. "Rhea, did you see that?" I whispered.

"What?" she said softly.

"Something big movin' along the hill."

"Sit quietly, son," Rhea said, but I had already whirled on the seat and was looking out the little window. I saw two riders bearing down on us—big men on big thoroughbreds.

"Faster, Rhea, faster! We may be able to outrun 'em." But Rhea pulled up, stopping the buggy with the men clattering up behind us.

A group of horsemen, dark shadows and shapes rising out of the land, sat across the road. Rhea talked to the nervous mare, calming her, settling her to a full stop. "Sit very still," she said to me. "Say nothing." She handed me the reins and reached for a cylinder of matches. Rhea lit the lantern we carried and hung it from the top of the frame. It threw a circle of light, revealing us to the riders and some of them to us—the two trailing us who now sat beside the buggy, the one who held the mare's head, and the leader who rode up on Rhea's side. They were Yankee soldiers.

"Evening, m'am," the lieutenant said.

"Good evening, Lieutenant," Rhea answered.

"May I ask where you are going, m'am?"

"Home," she said.

"Mighty cold to be out tonight. Where have you been?"

"My father was doctor here before his death. I still look in on his patients," Rhea said.

"Can you give me the name of the patient?" the young officer asked.

"I can give you a list of the patients if you like," she answered.

"The name of your last call will be sufficient," he said. My mouth was dry. He had us. We'd left Mrs. Graymer before four o'clock.

"Maude Pepper," Rhea said, without batting an eye. "She doesn't like strangers."

"This your boy?" he asked. She nodded. "You havent seen a peddler on the road have you, boy?"

"No, sir," I said. "I've been scrunched up trying to stay warm and eat my pound cake."

"You see a peddler, m'am?" he said.

"Soldier, the boy and I have told you where

100

we've been and why. It is plain you have no respect for our word. I'm tired and cold. I've been gone from home since daylight. I doctor people. That is a fact. I have my bag," she started to reach under the seat, but picked up the ether she'd put on the seat. "No, I have this. How many people ride about with ether?" Rhea opened the container. "Smell that. Ned Edgars keeps it in his store at Cane Hill. All he can get. Ask him. Can't get chloroform, no, not in this war." Rhea waved the ether about from rider to rider, backing them away. Finally, she thrust it at the lieutenant. He jumped back.

"M'am, be careful!"

"Careful!" She recapped it. "I'm too tired to be careful. If you have a reason to stop me further, state it."

"Very well, m'am. I suppose if you were smuggling—" he started to say.

"Smuggling!" Rhea said. "Find a woman and search me if I'm smuggling. I'm just trying to help stop some of the misery around here."

"I was sayin', if you were smuggling you'd have chloroform, not ether, and you'd be a whole lot more pleasant. Now, m'am, you stand in great danger being about at night. Should we meet again, and you do not have a paper permitting you to be out, stating your business, I'll take this buggy and put you under arrest. That is not an idle threat. Partisans and smugglers won't be tolerated."

"Can I get a paper at Fayetteville?"

"Yes, m'am."

"Very well, Lieutenant. I will get the paper. Thank you for the warning." Rhea took the reins, and we trotted through the soldiers. In a little while she blew out the lantern.

"Maude Pepper?" I asked.

Rhea smiled. "Mrs. Pepper has a fearful temper, boy, and a loyal heart. If the lieutenant lives past her gate, she'll tell him in detail about her rheumatiz and how much I help it."

In January there was a break in the weather—one of those spells of moderation that come to the mountains sometimes in winter. Rhea and I went to Fayetteville. It was a long trip to that county seat town. Fayetteville had a garrison of Federal troops so the stores there had things we could not buy closer to home. Rhea had other business there, too. She was worried about her husband. No letters had come from Jamie Dameron since late November. And ever since she was stopped by the Union patrol keeping martial law, which threatened to take her horse and buggy away, Rhea had wanted a paper allowing her to be on the roads at night. Since Rhea was the closest thing to a doctor our hills possessed, she had to be able to travel at any hour to the sick.

I had been to Fayetteville once before, but I was smaller then and that was before the war. It was a city set on hills looking south toward the blue haze of the Boston Mountains. The third most populous city in the state, it dazzled me with its size and bustle. Nearly a thousand people lived in the town, excluding the Federal troopers. There was Yankee money there and Yankee protection. The town was beginning to hum again with rebuilding. Fayetteville had been burned by the Confederates as they fell back from Pea Ridge the spring before. It had always been a town with strong Union sympathies. This, along with the shoddy treatment by the Confederates and the occupation of the city by Union troops, allowed the people to forget their southern patriotism sooner and begin to return to normal life earlier than the smaller towns which were unprotected and vulnerable to both Confederate guerrillas and Yankee renegades. In Fayetteville, there was

103

even talk of a coronet band to play on spring and summer evenings.

We took a room at Mrs. Able's lodging house and went up to the square where the burned out courthouse still lay in ruins but where there was a flurry of business around the stores and the Union and county offices. Rhea gave me a list of supplies and got me started at the store. She went off to do business with the Yankee captain of the garrison.

The store was in a brick building with high ceilings and a wide worn wooden stairway at the back that led up to a dentist's office and big items of merchandise like stoves and plows. Its interior was a miracle to me. I followed the clerk about as he filled our order. Each item seemed more amazing to me than the last. I peered through the shining glass cases and jars, at candy and fancy watches and pocket knives and gold-rimmed spectacles. The clerk's hand reached into the case I was studying and put two pair of the spectacles in our basket.

"That lady seemed too young for cheaters," he said.

"Ain't for her," I said. "They're for old Mrs. Winters and a man who lives near us, Edd Huggins."

"Nice of her to pick up for them," he said.

I started to say Rhea was a doctor and that was part of her job. But she'd told me never to say that. She said she was just a make-do healer and not to be taken for a trained physician. So I just nodded and said, "She's a nice person."

"Guess you all been hearing about the mystery marauder?" the clerk asked.

"Everybody knows about those tormentors," I said.

"No, boy," he said. "This one leaves flour or cornmeal or clothes or something good. A man came in here just this morning with money to pay his back bill. The boss had cut him off flat. Couldn't carry him anymore. But he had hard money to pay up. Said he found it setting in his wash basin on the porch in a tobacco pouch. The Yanks figured he stole it, but couldn't prove it. He ain't the first, neither. I heard a couple a men talking over there by the stove while I was putting up stock." I looked in the direction he pointed and tried to picture the men. "One of them found a long gun. He brought in some venison he'd shot with it and sold it."

"Who do you reckon it is?" I asked.

"No way of knowin'. But it's a pleasurable

105

thing for a change, wondering who might be out there doing good to folks instead of selling 'em out. Mighty pleasurable," the clerk said.

I hadn't noticed her come back but suddenly Rhea put her hand on my shoulder. "Clerk," she said. "This young fellow wants to pick out a good pocketknife. Can you help him out?"

I picked a fine big knife with three folding blades and a leather-punch. Rhea said it was a gift from Jamie Dameron. She wrote him about Sarah and me. She had a small bundle of letters from him and the traveling permit. Rhea was in fine spirits as we finished up with the store clerk.

Outside on the steps a crowd of men blocked our way. Their backs were to us, blocking the street. They were absorbed in watching some kind of altercation. Rhea wasn't interested and walked away down the boardwalk. I was caught between slipping in among the men and following her. I was not tied to her. I knew that. And she did not call me. I found a place at the rail by squirming through the men.

Two men I did not recognize were holding a third man while Jim Gilstrap, whom I'd seen at Eden's Bluff, pounded his fist into the man's

106

stomach. The man in the middle was already bloody about his face, but he wanted to talk.

"I tried to save 'em," he said, and Gilstrap hit him again, this time in the mouth.

"Shut your lyin' mouth," Gilstrap said. "Lyin' damn scum. You took 'em to the cave so they could be easy found."

"Why'd I fetch 'em a doctor, then?" the bloody man asked.

"Shut up," Gilstrap said and drew back his fist.

"Gilstrap, that's enough." The voice was not from one of the men on the steps or one of the Federal soldiers or their captain who watched from across the square. It belonged to Rhea Dameron. Gilstrap spun around.

"Stay out of this, Missus Dameron. Foard knows who told or he told the killers himself. Your standin' up for him out of kindness won't help that fact. The Grahams have a right to him. Two of their brothers died in that cave."

"I was in the cave. I'm alive. And I don't know who told about it," she said.

"That may well be, but you had a loss not a gain from it. When Frank Graham was killed, his woman moved in with Blackie Foard. Her and the place Graham owned belong to Foard now," Gilstrap said.

Rhea listened, seeming to turn over this possible motive of passion in her mind. "Foard," she said. "Did you profit from Frank Graham's death?"

Foard tried to shake off his holders and stand up straight. "Graham beat the woman all the time. I just felt sorry for her at first, then I got to care for her. I was not sorry when he died. He was deserving of it. But the other men were not, ma'am—not Doc Isaacs or the others. When the time to kill Graham come, I'd have done it myself—him and me, nobody else hurt. That's the truth."

"Move on! Don't bring your petty quarrels to these streets again," the Yankee captain said. "Buy what you came for and get out of town or I'll charge all of you. Sergeant, take that man to a doctor."

The men on the walk moved off amiably, satisfied with the day's entertainment. I caught up with Rhea, who was walking back toward the boarding house with the captain for supper. The captain was a big man, and my eyes were on a level with the huge horse pistol on his side.

The shine on that holster flap astounded me. I tried to walk as straight as the captain.

"Do you think it's a petty quarrel when men are going to kill each other, Captain Dwight?" Rhea asked.

"There's a lot of killing in wartime, Mrs. Dameron. A personal quarrel hardly seems important."

"But you keep the law here, personal quarrel or not."

"No, ma'am, I try to keep the law here. There is a difference. If I get in every little squabble I will not be able to handle the greater dangers to the security of the citizens. I don't have enough men for that."

"But shouldn't you handle even a personal quarrel when it's right before your eyes?" asked Rhea.

"I did. I stopped it," the captain said.

"But, Captain, you didn't stop it. You just changed the location. There have already been six deaths because someone betrayed the men in the cave. There will be more unless you find Crysop and the informer and deal with them," said Rhea.

"As far as I'm concerned, Crysop's partisans acted under wartime conditions, mopping up

109

Confederate bands. The informer did his duty in disclosing the location of the soldiers. He deserves our protection," Dwight said.

"Doesn't it matter to you that the men in that cave were severely wounded—not able to offer any resistance, let alone attack. They were Union men conscripted and shot by Confederate partisans in the first place. One of them, at least, was a valuable civilian. They were executed—a pistol stuck to their heads and the trigger pulled by men you know," Rhea said.

"I didn't see the bodies, Mrs. Dameron," said Dwight.

"I did," she said.

"Mrs. Dameron, I know your father was killed in the cave. I regret that, but circumstances sometimes dictate what appear to be cruel actions. Partisans operate under a different set of rules and purposes than regular military men. You know yourself about Quantrill and Anderson and the others of the Confederacy. Their main purpose is to keep our troops tied up in this area and away from the real fighting. Their other purpose is to terrorize people so badly they won't help us or join us. Can you blame us for putting out our own bands to perform the same function of intimidation against them? Can you blame us for using any tactic to get ourselves free of them, to bring this area into control so we can join our comrades fighting in the East and end the killing for good?" asked the captain.

"Yes, I can blame you," Rhea Dameron said. "Crysop's a killer, and you've commissioned him. You've made him legal against peaceful people who surely have a right to feed their families and care for their dying in this country, or we fight for nothing. You've done this when you are winning the war, Captain, not out of desperation. You've done it when you have a full army of regular soldiers in occupation, not when your army is being beaten half a country away. You've done this when you have a witness who will testify against him."

"A witness? What witness?" the captain asked.

"Me. I saw Crysop and his men come out of the cave at Eden's Bluff that morning. I saw him reholster his gun after killing my father. I heard this boy's father swear with his dying breath that Crysop did the killing himself," Rhea said. "Forgive me if I see no military purpose. I just see injustice. My sympathies are wholly with the Union. My husband is in that

111

army. But I will not accept Eleazar Crysop as a man necessary to our cause. He is a criminal, and by accepting his actions I become as criminal as he. Call him off, Captain. The people will believe you represent their hope, then, and they will help you. But they cannot go on fighting both sides. Let us tell people Crysop will stand trial for murdering the conscripts."

"It's really not that simple, Mrs. Dameron."

"It's that simple," Rhea said.

We could see the boarding house up the hill. We walked toward it in silence for some time. At last the captain asked Rhea if she was truly a doctor herself.

"No," Rhea said. "I'm a poor substitute for a physician, but I'm all there is west of here."

"Still you have some knowledge," the captain said.

"Yes."

"Well, I've been worrying about my stomach lately. It's probably nothing, of course, but still I wonder if it's common to experience sharp pains across here." He rubbed his hand across his midsection. "I've tried to keep it coated with milk and such, but sometimes it wakes me up. It's like being hit with a clenched fist, but a gripping, grinding pain." The captain put a lot of emphasis on the last two words.

"Your job probably puts you under a great deal of strain."

"Oh, yes, yes. I have to solve everybody's problems from the cook to the president," the captain agreed.

"Perhaps you could get away from your desk some. Ride out more and relax," Rhea suggested.

"But it's more than that. Sometimes I'm flighty and light-headed."

"What do you eat, captain?" Rhea asked.

"Well, Mrs. Dameron, I believe you are what you eat. I've been experimenting with several new eating regimens, trying to clean out all the poison from my body."

"Captain, eat good food and eat moderately. Your stomach will be very grateful and leave you at peace. Good day," Rhea said, and started up the stairs to the porch.

"Aren't you dining?" the captain asked.

"I have a nervous stomach myself tonight, Captain. And I have some long awaited letters to read," Rhea said, going through the door and toward the inner stairway.

"I have this sharp pain in my shoulder when

I do this," the captain said hastily. He lifted his right arm over his head and then back. "Oh, oh," he muttered as pain streaked across his round face.

"Try not to do that then," Rhea said, and took me by the shoulder up the stairs.

"Rhea," I said when we were alone. "What's wrong with his stomach?"

"John Luke, the Yankee captain has an ancient, but fairly common disorder. At our first meeting over the travel permit, he discovered I knew some medicine. The news transformed a healthy man into a mass of symptoms—a strange fleeting pain in his chest and right arm, a vicious shooting pain in his back and legs after twelve hours in the saddle." She imitated his movements. "My God, if he didn't have a pain after twelve hours in a saddle, I would be worried."

Rhea and I had a tray of things from the kitchen in her room. Afterwards I went to bed in Mrs. Able's boy's room. The next morning we returned to Lord's Vineyard. Rhea seemed to have put her conversation with the captain aside. After reading her letters, she was full of plans for planting, cleaning, and cooking. Jamie Dameron was coming home in the spring.

7

LORD'S VINEYARD was now my home. I awakened each morning with new places to discover, new trails to follow through the foot-deep leaves of the woods above the house. In a short time, I learned the land around the place. I tagged after Rhea whenever I became bored with exploring or when I became curious about what she was doing. Increasingly I found myself wanting to be with adults. Their conversation fascinated me. It was full of new things I suddenly wanted to learn. Rhea worked with Sarah and me on our schoolin'. She showed me books that opened the doors of adventures— *Ivanhoe, David Copperfield, Leatherstocking Tales.* She set no limits on my hungry mind, allowing me to read whatever I could grasp. I began to hang about her little dispensary more and more. I was perplexed by the mystery of what she saw and felt that I could not see at all. I asked questions, hundreds of questions. She tried to show me. She brought me her father's anatomy book, and I started to learn the complex and alien Latin names.

Rhea was not like anyone I had met. She intrigued me with her knowledge and independence—traits I did not expect in a woman. She was a paradox I studied carefully—a bold woman who would beard a Yankee captain on justice and listen patiently to the most ignorant of human beings who came with illness to her door. In that valley she was life to us all—the energy that sustained us and met our needs! When Rhea was away the valley was empty. I came to dread her absence, when I was left to listen to Claudia run on about morals and manners, to help Hillary with routine chores, to play children's games with Sarah. But it was Claudia Isaacs who made me first think about Rhea's larger role beyond our hidden valley—Claudia and the fact that Rhea never let me go with her at night. Many times I heard her leave the house and ride across the creek to leave Vineyard. But she never once asked me to come along as she often did on mild days.

When February brought more cold weather to the mountains, we were forced indoors by the fire. I sat at the parlor table, looking at Jones and Quain's *Anatomy*, a bulky tome that

I could not support comfortably on my lap. The pictures of bones and human organs interested me enough to struggle with the words. Rhea helped me for a while, but she seemed restless and soon left me to look out the window down the long wide valley. Hillary and Claudia chatted and sewed, with their feet propped on little stools to save them from the drafts on the floor. Sarah played with Joey by the fire.

"What are you worrying about, Rhea?" Hillary asked.

"I'm just wondering if the Andersens have enough cornmeal. I know they didn't get a crop last year with their man away."

"Why, what good is worrying going to do you?" Claudia said. "There's not a blessed thing you can do for them without robbing us. I'd think six mouths would be enough for you to worry about." Claudia Isaacs never had enough. Beautiful as she was, she sought to be more beautiful, to be told of her beauty. Well cared for by Rhea's provision, she never had enough to eat and certainly not enough to share.

"I'm not worrying, Claudia. I'm wondering what that family is doing. We could be in their position very easily ourselves."

117

"I don't think about such things," Claudia said. "They just make you unpleasant and poor company. Besides, we could never be like the Andersens. They're just plain trash."

"The Andersens are poor, but they work hard. And they were beginning to prosper a little before the war. I don't think they are trash," Rhea said.

"I do," Claudia said emphatically. "Dela Andersen isn't even his legal wife. They just took up, Louise Mapain said. Why Dela doesn't even wear a proper petticoat when she comes over here for your free care."

"What's a proper petticoat?" Rhea asked, smiling.

"Well," Claudia thought a moment. "It's full enough to cover your nakedness. And it has some refinement to it. Dela Andersen's petticoat is just feed sacks bleached out and stitched on a band."

Rhea said, "It's feed sacks, but it is clean."

"Clean! Clean is all I hear, and it is not everything, Rhea. Besides, what have we to spare anymore? You give every old troll who comes to that back door anything I don't hide."

"You don't have an extra petticoat, do you?" Rhea asked, her eyes twinkling.

"I most certainly do, and it's not to be given away or made into bandages."

"I'd think Christian charity would compel you to share your petticoats," Rhea said meekly.

"If you want Dela Andersen to have a petticoat, give her one of yours," Claudia said in a huff. Joey was getting cross and he bellowed at her grating voice. "My God, it's time to feed him again." Claudia left the room with Joey.

"I bet the milk curdles in his poor little mouth," Hillary said. "It's a two-hour ride to the Andersen's place."

Rhea nodded. "I can leave after supper sometime and be back by morning."

"I'll get the meal after supper and bring it to the barn. You want me to get one of her petticoats?" Hillary asked.

"No. They belong to Claudia. I'll find one of mine," Rhea said.

"It may be quite a hunt for you, as fast as they are disappearing into bandages."

Suddenly I was aware of some mystery shared by Rhea and Hillary, denied to Claudia and us children. I slipped from my chair. In the kitchen I opened the meal drawer. Claudia was right, there was not much meal in the house, not enough to make a four-hour ride worth while to the rider or the recipient. In fact, I had never seen the meal drawer full or empty. It was always the same, enough for a day or two's supply. Yet Hillary was going to bring it after supper to the barn. For the past two months at Vineyard I had seen Rhea give food, medicine, blankets even, to a dozen people who came to the farm. Yet we always had enough for the family. I had never seen her buy quantities of anything. Somewhere at Vineyard, I realized, there was food and other things hidden. I decided to follow Hillary after supper.

I endured supper with the repeated promise to myself of the adventure to come. Claudia and Rhea dallied over their food. Sarah had a second helping. Finally we all finished and cleared away the dishes. Rhea and Claudia finally went to the parlor, and Sarah and I took our places at the lesson table. Glancing up from my *McGuffey's*, I could see Rhea reading. I heard Hillary in the kitchen. I gave up reading and tried to copy one of the anatomical drawings, but I was preoccupied, listening for the sound of the back door. When Hillary went out tonight she was not going to throw out the scraps. At last I heard the faint closing of the door. I casually shut my book.

"I want a drink," I said.

"Me, too," Sarah said.

I leaned over and whispered through gritted teeth, "No, you don't." Sarah returned to her book. Neither Rhea nor Claudia looked up as I left the room.

From the shadows of the back porch, I could see Hillary leaning into her climb up the face of the hill toward the east stream. She went into the woods and disappeared. In a cat's blink I was off the porch and following her.

By the time I reached the woods, I was winded. I leaned against a tree, looking for her in the darkness, listening for any sound. In a few minutes I heard the leaves crunch close to the creek. My eyes found Hillary as she waded into the shallow water and walked heavily up the stream. I could not tell where she was headed, for a great slab of rock seemed to end the path abruptly. I saw her walk then into a black shadow. She was gone.

I waited a moment and left my resting place to follow her. The water froze me as it came over the tops of my shoes and soaked my socks. I drew in my breath and made my way toward the mysterious shadow where I had last seen Hillary.

In the moonlight, I saw a broad slit of light. It was the meeting place of two rocky slabs that overlapped with a hallway between. I had not made discovery in my explorations because whenever I entered this wood someone had called me. I now knew that was no accident. I stepped into the shadow and followed the stream and rock wall. My hand felt the wall turn abruptly to the right, and I followed, stepping out of the stream on a rocky bank.

Suddenly I was knocked to the ground, and someone was on top of me. I struggled. Hillary's voice said, "Lay still, you Satan."

The next I knew Rhea's voice said from behind me, "Let him up."

Hillary stood up, and I got onto my knees. Rhea lit a lantern, sitting on a stone shelf. As the light spread through the room, I saw I was in a kind of natural manger. Shallow caves in the hills are often used by farmers as animal shelters. Someone had fixed this one up with a log-feed trough and rigged a pole gate of sorts across the entrance. It would be a good stable with plenty of feed and water.

"I heard him in the leaves," Hillary said. "Little pitchers have big ears."

"Yes," said Rhea. "It wasn't your fault. John Luke, do you know where you are?"

"In a manger cave," I said.

"Why did you follow Hillary?"

"I figured you had a secret hiding place, and I wanted to know," I said.

"Why didn't you ask us?" Rhea asked.

"I don't know. I didn't think about it. I guess I wanted to do something that would be exciting, an adventure like in those story books you give me," I said.

"John Luke, you must think before you act. Ask me if you want to know anything. I will tell you the truth. Don't ever take on an adventure you haven't thought through. It's dangerous to you and to all of us. Do you see that?"

"It didn't hurt anyone," I said.

"It could have hurt you if Hillary had used her knife. It can hurt us all if you make a slip to anyone about this cave." I didn't say anything back to Rhea, but I felt pretty low. "Come with me," Rhea said.

Rhea opened one end of the manger rack and slipped behind. I followed her. Blanket curtains covered the manger back and hid the lantern's light from anyone outside. A natural stone hallway ran into the darkness before her. She walked swiftly down the passageway and into a side room.

She lifted the lantern high, revealing an interior piled with produce and plunder. I learned that night that for three years, she and her father and husband had hidden medicine and food here from the roving bands of partisans. Using the Yankee currency her husband sometimes sent, they had bought certain things from the speculators and hid their supplies in the cave. The produce from a garden back in the flat land above the cave supplemented what was stored here from the farm and town gardens. A field of summer poppies had yielded an opium that could be used when other pain killers were gone. Medical herbs, neatly bundled and dried, hung on racks. There were sacks of wool and cotton, cornmeal and flour. There was straw and blankets and powder and bullets. And there was a small bag of coins in a tobacco pouch.

There were other rooms further back along the twisting hall. Each was filled with the family's and the doctor's necessaries. So this was the source of the items that mysteriously appeared on the back porches of the hill people. Citizens hereabouts had long speculated about the night rider, took it as a sign that somewhere decency still lived even in hard times. The idea of the mysterious provider sustained them in a way that the quickly eaten food or spent coins did not. It gave them hope; faith that for all the robbers there was still a kind of ragged justice. The great mystery of where the things came from was solved. The solution seemed so obvious now. Who better than Rhea, who went about freely as a healer, who knew the needs of people intimately?

"John Luke, this is not to be mentioned to anyone at any time. Not to Hillary or to me either. Under no circumstances are you to speak of what you've seen here. Nor are you to come here alone," Rhea said. "You are not to reveal this cave, whatever happens, no matter how bad."

8

AFTER that night, I still heard Rhea Dameron leave the stone barn and ride into the biting winter morning, but I was warm and secure in my bed, comforted by a secret knowledge that Rhea was going to do good. In my child's mind that good deed was her armor, her protection against the evil that rode up and down our land. In fact, I believed the good works of Rhea Dameron were the reason God or whoever governed the senseless events of life and war kept Lord's Vineyard safe from the perils that fell on our neighbors. I mentioned this to Rhea once. "My God, boy," she said. "You scare me to death. If Lord's Vineyard's safety depends on my good works, they'll burn us out tonight!"

Because the journey to church in town was long and tedious, we regularly joined ourselves in worship in the parlor of Sabbath mornings. At first, I loathed these occasions of prayer and reading and stillness. I resented the Sunday clothes that bound me and immoblized my body in a straight chair. But being shut up on a hill farm could take a toll on anyone. As days dragged by in natural succession, I came to look forward to the women's enthusiasm for worship.

On Saturday, the house fairly hummed with activity. The house itself was put in order. Anything unmade, unswept, unscrubbed, or undusted from Friday was polished off before nine o'clock. Then the cooking began. Eggs were ordered from the barn and spring house. Sarah and I ripped old hens gingerly from their nests to find white or brown orbs. We returned to the house with baskets and hats full, anticipating cakes and pies made with molasses. Sugar was too dear. We hung about Rhea, watching her bust the shells with one swift hand. We watched the golden sun of yolk slip through the jagged crack and plop into the waiting hill of flour. Before it sunk into the little Vesuvius, Rhea's wooden spoon hurtled it around the giant bowl. We waited, anticipating the summons to lick that bowl when the main contents filled pans and sat waiting in the oven.

After the cake bowl and before Claudia could cut my hair, I headed for the barn to watch with gruesome interest as Hillary assassinated a chicken for our Sunday lunch. The curious habit of headless chickens running about never failed to amaze me, no matter how Rhea explained it. I'd watch Hillary boil the corpse and grab bunches of feathers until the bird stood naked. Her swift knife dissected it effortlessly at the joints, slipped into the empty body cavity and split the fowl asunder.

I returned with Hillary to the kitchen to find the cakes golden brown, cooling. My interest in the icing operation provoked several, "It's not cool enough yet" responses. Finally Rhea abandoned any answers and countered with an inquiry about the completion of my chores. Leaving Hillary, she and I went to the barn where water pails were scrubbed, stalls cleaned and filled with sweet straw, hay and feed checked, horses curried, sheep combed for mats and mud. All the farm work stopped on Sunday except the feeding. Our animals enjoyed the day of rest as much as their master, perhaps more. By the time we returned to the house, lunch was on the table, the cake sat iced, and the bowl waited for a swift cleaning of the tasty globs that clung to spoon and sides.

Each Saturday afternoon, I brought in wood and finished any chores while the women cleaned the kitchen and saw to our clothes. They washed their long lustrous hair and bathed. Water was heated in the kitchen—two large teakettles full—and carried to a little room where Jamie Dameron had installed a small copper tub. There the boiling water was mixed with the cold spring water into a comfortable bath. I was the last to plunge beneath the flood, generally under threat from Rhea to help me.

Sunday we rose early, ate a good breakfast, performed our minimal chores, dressed, and took our places in the parlor. Rhea read from the Bible. I liked Noah and Jonah and all the young King David stories. I think Rhea enjoyed reading the adventure parts of the Old Testament for she eagerly skipped over the "begats" to get to them. She prayed then, for us and her husband. Rhea was always thankful in those short prayers, too. She amazed me sometimes at what she was thankful for; I think she was mostly thankful things were not worse.

Some Sundays we had visitors, our neighbours. I liked Walter England and his family best. Walter helped us with plowing and harvest. They were Quakers. At first, they seemed peculiar with their silence and thee's and thou's. But they never prayed long, and

129

the silent worship they required had a kind of pleasant feel. They always brought something to eat to our table, making it richer. I liked playing with their boy after lunch. George was good company.

On the other hand, I always dreaded Mr. Edd Huggins. Edd lived three miles away over the hill. He was a great coon hunter, but unlike most hunters he was talkative. He had the look of distance in his eyes. His head was always cocked for the bay of hounds. His prayers were so long he sometimes forgot the sense of his sentence. He would struggle around awhile before he gave up and started a new thought. His strategy was to wear God out, just plain wear down the Divinity with a complete summary of every event in our county's history since Huggins' last prayer. As near as I could tell, this was not since his last visit to our Sunday table.

Rhea tuned out on his prayers after the first ten minutes. She was a believer, true in heart, but, at least once. I know she went sound to sleep. Hillary had to shake her awake for lunch. Huggins didn't seem to mind when Rhea explained how comforting his words were and how his voice mesmerized her.

She never mentioned the nocturnal venture that had left her half-asleep anyway. After all the praying, Huggins was ready for lunch spelled with a capital chicken. It was Huggins who prayed for the soul of Sam Foard, and, thus, informed us of his demise. After lunch I heard him and Rhea talking.

"Hanged him. They just caught him comin' down the road and hanged him," Huggins said.

"Do you know who did it?" Rhea asked.

"Why Gilstrap or the Grahams, I reckon," answered Huggins. "There ain't one of the Foards safe now. Blackie's the one they really want, but he's over in the Indian country."

"Do you think Blackie betrayed the conscripts?"

"Don't know, Rhea. Don't really matter much either. There's them that believes it so strong no evidence would persuade them. They got it in their craws, and they ain't goin' to be happy till they spit it out. It flat galls the Grahams that woman took up with Blackie."

"I don't think Foard did it," Rhea said. "I think Gilstrap is after the wrong man."

Huggins just picked his teeth and thought. "Don't matter none anyways, I guess. There's a time for all things—a time to kill . . . and

131

this here is it. The killing time is here," he said, and walked on off across the hill with his two bony hounds trotting loosely at his heels.

"Why doesn't it matter?" I asked.

"I don't know," Rhea said. "Maybe there are just times when killing doesn't have to have a reason. People just want to kill."

Sunday services had a salutary effect on my life—the strong vivid pictures of the Bible heroes, the gentle healing and spirit of the Nazarene gave me men to imitate. By turns I was strong old Sampson killing his enemies with the jawbone of an ass, and gentle Jesus turning the other cheek. It was hard for me to hold a center course. My growing conviction that the safety of our valley depended on appeasing God with good works motivated my interest in spiritual things. Finally I announced my conversion to Rhea on Tuesday as we drove into town.

"Rhea," I said. "I've decided to be a Christian. I think my ma and God would like it."

"That's fine, John Luke. It's good to choose your path early," she said and drove on. I had expected more from Rhea. At church in town, the redeemed were welcomed with warm handshakes and hugs and "Praise God's!" She seemed neutral.

"I'm not going to cuss anymore," I said. "Or be mean to Sarah. I'm changed. I'm going to be good, good as pie."

Rhea drove on, looking steadily at the road. "Reckon what good is?" she said.

"Why it's not doing anything wrong!" I said in surprise.

"Do you suppose you can know every bit of what's good and what's bad right away, John Luke?"

"I sure hope so because I aim to be good. I'm going to do my damn . . . my best. God'll have respect for what I've done."

"You're using 'I' a lot," Rhea said. "You best let God have a hand, too, son. We don't make ourselves, and we don't make ourselves all at once. We just grow slowly one direction or another, slipping and falling, crawling back under his keeping power."

"I thought you'd be pleased," I said.

"I am pleased you've begun, John Luke. But you are in a precarious place as a new believer —you are caught in the current of enthusiasm and short on an anchor. Discouragement and backsliding come easy then. Just give God a chance to shape you instead of trying to do it all yourself. He's already begun, boy; and when you fall down, he'll still be right there wanting you back. Listen more to God than men. Listen more than tell, son, that's the secret. Don't take a human being for God. They all fall down working out their lives. Don't hate God for the bad men you'll meet. They chose their own way when they had a better choice."

When we reached Prairie Grove, I hopped off the buggy at the blacksmith shop. Before long I was idling around the forge, pushing this and that, listening to the iron sizzle as Lloyd Barnes put it in the water. "Get away from there," Barnes said. "This ain't no playpen for a baby. Go on outside."

I sauntered out, taking my time, not showing my hurt feelings. Down the street I could see Rhea's buggy. Lloyd Barnes, Jr. was messing around the horse. She was tossing her head and trying to back up. Like David I saw my Goliath. Barnes was a foot taller and two years older. But righteousness was my armor. I ran down the street, stopped, and walked purposefully down the sidewalk till I was on the porch, looking down at Junior.

"Let the horse alone," I said.

"You ain't big enough to make me," Junior said.

"Junior," I said. "I'm a Christian. I ain't supposed to hit folks or cuss. But you are doing a bad thing pestering that horse. And I believe if you think about it you'd stop."

"Kiss my foot," Junior said. "You're just a titty baby, scared up by a bunch of silly women, taggin' around that prissy Missus Dameron. Lily." He said "lily" like it was the nastiest thing there was to be.

"You have gone too far, Junior. You have called me and my friends names. I will show you who is a lily. I will come down from here and thrash you."

I didn't say anymore, for Junior Barnes pulled me off the porch and started thumping my head on the boards. He was still at it when I saw Rhea's boots beside my face. Junior let go and ran away toward the smithy. I tried to shake my brain back into place as Rhea got in the buggy.

"Ain't you going to do anything?" I said, climbing in beside her.

"Yes," she said taking my head between her hands and studying the bump rising there. "I'm going to give you some good advice. I heard what you said to Junior. You told him you were a Christian and acted like you were better than

135

him because of it. I personally wouldn't do that again. Next you told him you were going to fight him. That warned him, and he thrashed you. When you're not as big as your adversary, you sure shouldn't give him the advantage of a warning, too. If you plan to hit anyone in the future, keep your mouth shut. That's advice I believe your father would stand behind." Rhea clucked up the horse, and we drove off through town.

"Ain't you mad 'cause I said I was a Christian and got in a fight. 'Cause I'm a hypocrite."

"Animals fight, men reason things out, John Luke. I hope you'll remember that. But we live in a hard world, and I cannot tell you you should never fight. I wish I could believe that as firmly as our Quaker friends. It seems to me there are times when the choice is between two evils, fighting or giving in to wrong. No one can tell you what to do then."

I slumped against the side of the buggy, holding my head and wondering how such good plans had come to this.

The road home excited little interest from me so I dozed and nursed my head until Rhea stopped the buggy. Looking up, I saw Dela Andersen pushing a kind of cart heaped high with bedding, household goods, and children. Dela herself was a bony woman with deep set eyes. Like many hill women of that generation, she was old at thirty. Deep lines cut through her gaunt face. There was no flesh to her or even on her smallest baby. They all had a starved and haggard look that no amount of food could ever conceal. Starvation had taken something, some confidence or hope, that they would never find again. There would always be that resignation to defeat, the resignation that would never question or challenge their ability to change themselves or their world. They were people carried by the tide; afloat still, but without control of their destinies.

We were used to that look in those days. We were used to families taking up stakes and moving on. The war had made it worse because it was women without men, with just children and a pitiful load of household goods moving up to Missouri or even on to Texas where they could find food and some security against the guerrilla bands and wait for men who might never return. We saw these women refugees from hard times every day in the war, packed up and moving.

"Mrs. Andersen," Rhea said. "Where are you going?"

"Up to Missouri," Dela Andersen said, "my man's got kinfolk up there says they'll let us stay awhile with them. I thought we might have stayed here longer, but our food's near gone. Raiders come yesterday and took all the meal we had and the stock. There was Yank soldiers with them. Ain't no help there. There's no hope, Missus Dameron. I got six kids and ain't one of 'em old enough to help plow or nothing. I got three dollars a month to feed us. I spent the last five days walkin' tryin' to buy food. Them that made a crop won't sell for speculation. They won't sell me corn for two dollar a bushel when they can get thirty from a whiskey-still man. I'm so tired I can hardly lift my hand to this here cart. There's no hope, just more of the same ahead. More and more till a body gives up livin' and lays down to die."

"There is hope," Rhea said. "You must not give up, Mrs. Andersen."

Dela Andersen smiled at Rhea. "There's hope for a lady like you, but there ain't hope for no woodsy like me. I'm ignorant born and bred, and I'll die that way," Dela Andersen said. "I thank ye for what you done for me and my youngins, but it was for nothing."

"It was not for nothing," Rhea said. "You were going to make it. You had your kids started proper and your farm was good. Those damn raiders took it from you. You remember that. You are good people, Mrs. Andersen. You aren't beat. You go on to Missouri now and rest. Don't worry about your future. Your farm will still be here when the war's over. I'll look about it. It's waitin' for you. Hope on that, Mrs. Andersen. Let's put something in those empty buckets on your cart." Then Rhea got down and went around back of the buggy. She opened the flour sack and poured half the contents into the empty buckets Dela Andersen brought. "This isn't much," Rhea said, "but it will get you to Missouri. You know there's a camping place where women join up for the journey outside Fayetteville. If you stop there you'll be safe for the night. It's on the Gillespie farm, and they are good people." Rhea and I helped Mrs. Andersen load up a few more things on the cart and watched as the family started along the winding rut road. Rhea ran to her with a last question.

"Did you know the partisans who raided your farm?"

Dela Andersen looked straight in Rhea Dameron's eyes. "Crysop," she said.

140

9

THE Gillespie farm accumulated women refugees, dislocated by the war and bent on joining with other women to move on to greater safety. I do not know that it was ever thought out or organized, although an effort was made to relieve the suffering of soldiers' families by citizens' committees in many cities in the South. But as border people we were not so blessed—there was just not a pervasive sense of being Yank or Reb, and by 1863 we were pretty much in Union hands. For poor women whose husbands had the misfortune of being recruited into the Confederate army in 1861 and 1862, there was not much hope. The Confederates did not care for them in Union Arkansas, and their husbands were away in the East defending the old South.

Toward the end, Arkansas men deserted the Confederate ranks without qualm, often in groups, tired of fighting for the rich planters while their own wives and children were left to starve, to suffer the repeated attacks of guerrilla

141

bands. It seemed plain to them that they were fighting for political interests other than their own. They spat on allegiances beyond their farm and family. They had, after all, been tricked and exploited and used by political men. Our people lost their innocence in that war, and it would be a long time before their bitterness died. But the Union women fared little better without men to make their crops and guerrillas terrorizing them.

In late winter and early spring, before new crops could be planted was the worst time—the starve-out time when women made their way to Gillespie's farm. From there they moved out toward Ft. Smith and Texas; others headed toward Missouri across burned out Pea Ridge and Wilson's Creek. They lived at the farm in tents or shanties they built of scavenged board or pieces of metal. They moved into any outbuilding, and finally the Gillespies opened their barn to the refugee women.

This natural gathering place, then, became a kind of institution the women learned about, a destination for their first feeble steps toward a better life. Some of the late-comers turned up boards against the side of a standing shed and huddled there with their children. There was much sickness from exposure and poor sanitation, enteritis, measles, respiratory disorders, malaria in summer and fall if they stayed that long. There were also the special sicknesses of women and children, particularly childbirth and malnutrition.

Rhea, of course, was drawn toward these unfortunate women. Generally, she spent one or two whole days each week there, more if the trouble was unusual. After I'd recovered from my smallpox vaccination, she sometimes took me along. I was useful, I think, to Rhea, a kind of spy. I could sometimes get information from the children that their proud mothers would not always reveal.

Some of the women were educated and of means before the war. Others were not. These last desperate ones determined me to study, and, years later, to educate my own daughters, for I saw their needless suffering was nourished by their ignorance. They held to horrifying beliefs and remedies, for example. Rhea fought those beliefs, but they died hard and many times took the believer with them. Many expecially gruesome remedies surrounded childbirth.

Rhea and I arrived early at the farm and said

143

hello to the Gillespies. They were an older couple who had raised a large family of their own, a family split apart by the war. Mrs. Gillespie had a sharp eye for sickness. Before we had had a cup of herb tea, she described the worst cases. One of the Fayetteville doctors had vaccinated for smallpox a few days before and there was a general reaction to that, but Mrs. Gillespie and some of the other women had that under control. Her principal concern was a woman expecting a child who had walked almost fifty miles out of the hills alone. When she arrived, she had eaten nothing but black walnuts for more than a week. Rhea and I went with Mrs. Gillespie down toward the tents and lean-tos. Knowing Rhea, I sat down outside the shack and did not offer to go inside. In a little while she'd want me to build a fire or fetch water or something. I liked to be handy.

Inside the hovel was the sick woman, a granny woman, Mrs. Gillespie, and Rhea. Rhea wasn't tall, but she could not stand up straight inside. The sick woman lay on a kind of cot, covered with dirty quilts and a thin army blanket. I saw Rhea touch her forehead and then pull down the skin under her eye. She bent her head over the woman's chest and listened.

The sick woman never spoke or moved. She just lay there, staring at the ceiling. But the granny woman talked fast, only much of what she said not too complementary to Rhea or the patient.

"You'd best get out," she said. "I done what I kin, but she's bound to die for her sins, deserves to for all her sins."

Rhea looked up but didn't say anything to the granny. I saw her pull back the covers and gently begin to examine the sick woman's abdomen. She talked to her softly, but I could not hear because the old woman kept chattering.

"I put a axe under the bed to cut her pains, and I got the snuff for the quillin' 'cause that baby won't want to come. Ashamed to. Bet on that," the granny said. Quilling was a drastic means of compelling a strong contraction. A turkey quill filled with snuff was blown into the patient's nose. The paroxysm of sneezing which followed, propelled the fetus quickly through the birth canal. The sin the baby was ashamed of was the mother's resort to prostitution to stay alive.

Rhea covered the woman and came outside with Mrs. Gillespie. "Is there room for her in the barn?" Rhea said. "She'll surely die down here. Her time is very near but her body won't stand the birthing. If we can get get Dr. Hill from Fayetteville maybe he can take the child."

Mr. Gillespie went into town for the surgeon, Dr. Hill. Rhea set much faith on her father's former friend. Meanwhile, Rhea and Mrs. Gillespie found a place for the sick woman in the barn and moved her. They washed her, which greatly offended the granny woman and the crowd she'd begun to gather about her. They fed the sick woman broth, trying to build up her meager strength. A surgeon other than Dr. Hill arrived in late afternoon.

Dr. Jonathan Pruett was a contract surgeon for the army. He was a tall stern man, arrogant in his knowledge, resentful of the request to return to the farm. Rhea did not care for him, always requested another physician when she sent for help. But she spoke civilly. He did not return Rhea's greeting, but followed Mrs. Gillespie into the stall where the sick woman rested. He did not even go to the bed, but stopped in the entrance.

"I saw this woman yesterday," he said. "I told you then it was hopeless. And you've wasted my time calling me back out here."

146

"Perhaps if you do a Caesarean you can save her and the child," Rhea said.

"Where did you take your training?" Pruett asked. Rhea's jaw tightened. "It is hopeless, a waste of valuable time when there are so few doctors and so many who can be saved."

Rhea spoke softly, but I knew she was beginning to boil. "It is never a waste of time to help someone, Doctor." The first words had opened a floodgate. Mrs. Gillespie pulled Rhea's arm in a signal to stop, but it was too late. "No doubt you developed your philosophy on the battlefield, Doctor. But I suspect your training consisted of a few weeks in a school specializing in diplomas. You contracted out to see the sights and try your hand at cutting. Stop me if I'm wrong, Doctor. Since then you've learned to cut and carve the living into the dying for your hundred dollars a month besides the fees you extort from these women. You've never read a medical paper, never looked through a microscope. Your first dissection was on the field. You prescribe a dose of opium for looseness or a dose of calomel for tightness. You never wash your hands unless they are sticky or smell. You wipe your instruments on your

147

apron. You don't know medicine, Doctor. You're a barber."

Mrs. Gillespie said something to Rhea and she spoke back to her. "At least a few people out here would be better off if he never came back. Some of them might even be alive, unlike the Tillis boy." Rhea had been upset about Pruett's treatment of the boy, and now her feelings had focused in an accusation. "Did you ever sit with an eight-year-old while he died of gangrene, Doctor?"

Pruett stomped out of the barn nearly knocking me flat. He threw his bag in the buggy and gave the horse a startling pop with the whip. That was all we saw of him.

"Hurrah!" I said, caught up in the eloquence of Rhea's words.

"Hush, boy," she said. "That little speech was fool-hardy and very expensive for the sick people out here." Rhea said quietly, almost to herself, "God help us." She went to the sick woman then. She talked with her while she wiped her forehead with a wet towel. I heard the woman say, "Do it."

Rhea and Mrs. Gillespie went to work, boiling Rhea's instruments, washing down a table and the floor in the tack room with sodium hypochloride and lye soap to stop the "noxious effluvia" and to sanitize where they would work. Then Rhea and Mrs. Gillespie washed their hands and the sick woman's stomach in chlorinated water, a procedure which Rhea's father had heard of from Germany. The women bound clean aprons over their bodies. Mrs. Gillespie administered the chloroform, and Rhea did the cutting.

After a while, Mrs. Gillespie emerged with the baby. It was dead. I opened the door and saw Rhea sitting on a crate with her head in her hands. The woman on the table was neatly covered but still unconscious. I went to Rhea and put my arm around her shoulders.

"You tried," I said. "You did your best."

Rhea hugged me. Then she said with anger low in her voice, "Our best just isn't good enough." She went down the hallway and out into the yard.

"Murderer!" the granny woman said. "High and mighty she-male doctor. Childkiller!" And the women with her took up the cry. Rhea didn't respond, she just looked at them, at the red anger that twisted their faces. Finally she said, "I won't argue with you." She walked off

149

toward the creek, the wind whipping her unbuttoned coat about her.

Mrs. Gillespie, however, had a few words to say. "You fools. You ignorant fools. That child was already dead, putrifying in the poor woman, who's still alive thanks to Rhea. Without that woman a dozen women and children at this farm alone in the past six months would have died. She comes when the men can't or won't. When the weather's freezin'. Anytime of day or night. She's never taken a penny for her skill. She's paid for your medicine. She's never catered to your superstitions, but she's cared for you. And that's more than some." Mrs. Gillespie stared at the granny woman till she went off with two or three of the other crones.

Rhea's patient lived somehow, maybe just because Rhea and Mrs. Gillespie wanted her to so badly, as they sat with her through the long night and cared for her in the coming days. No real trouble occurred because of Dr. Pruett. The patient lived and Mrs. Gillespie knew the child was born dead. There just was not much to say about the incident, and not much concern since it involved the lost women. But because of Rhea, I was exposed to a point of view I might never have known, and in later years, I was glad of it.

The war affected women in many ways, making some strong and independent, some weak and pitiful, others mean and greedy. One of the strangest phenomenon was the corn women. They boiled into our country, heading south to beg food from the planters, the rich folks in the deep part of the state away from raiders, people with Negroes to plant crops. Each of these women had a paper from a judge stating that she was indigent. As soldiers' wives and widows, they supposedly were owed the support of those fortunate enough to have food. Their route was southerly, but we came to know them in the northern counties first.

I saw them when they came over the ridge at Maude Pepper's. I sat on the porch watching the strange sight. There were maybe ten of the creatures coming down the hill. Some were clustered together, but others were separated from the main group, like outriders or scouts. Each was bundled in rags of clothing over rags of clothing. They carried homemade sacks three or four feet long. As they neared the house, the flankers spread out toward the outbuildings, and they all began to tumble run down toward the cabin. I yelled for Rhea. She and Mrs. Pepper and I watched the corn women descend.

"What you make of this, Rhea?" Mrs. Pepper said.

"I don't know," Rhea answered. "But it doesn't feel right, does it?"

Mrs. Pepper stepped back in the cabin and returned with a double-barreled shotgun. We waited quietly for the women, who slowed their run to a walk at sight of the gun.

"Good day to ya," the dusty spokeswoman said, smiling through rotten teeth at us standing on the porch.

Mrs. Pepper said, "Day."

"We be goin' south lookin' for food to take back home to our starvin' chillurn and old folk. We shore are tared and lookin' for a place to rest up 'fore we go back to the river."

"No doubt your run down my hill tuckered you out some," Mrs. Pepper said. The corn woman studied us and the house and kind of signalled another pair of women who dropped off out of the group and started around the back. "Stay where you stand," said Maude Pepper.

"We got papers sayin' we're in-digent and

152

needin' food and whatever else ya kin spare," the leader said, pulling out a wrinkled paper from her coat and smoothing it on her thigh with her hand in fingerless gloves. "If ya kin read."

"I can read," said Mrs. Pepper. "But there's little here for sale or giveaway. I'm a widow woman myself knowing hard times. I've a mite of cornmeal mush and some sorghum for your supper if that will help you. There's a couple of pounds of blackeyed peas I can spare. If any of you are of a mind to, I've some scraps and cotton I was saving up to make a quilt. You're welcome to it. I won't need it. And I've feathers from my old ducks that would make up into fine pillows."

"I'll come inside and have a look," said the leader woman, starting toward the cabin porch.

"I'll bring it out," said Maude Pepper. She handed Rhea the shotgun and said softly, "See they wait, girl."

Rhea and I stood on the porch looking down at the women. They'd inched closer during the conversation. It was plain now they were an unwashed lot with greasy hair, dirty spots on their hands and faces, and filthy clothing. One had sores on her face around the mouth. She

153

was stroking the buggy horse and working her way slowly down the animal's back toward the buggy.

"You must be a rich lady havin' a fine horse and buggy like this," the diseased woman said. Rhea didn't answer.

"Your bag's in there and the rifle," I said. Rhea nodded.

Maude Pepper came out with the things she'd promised. She sat them on the step. The women surged up and started to go through them. I saw one grab up a child's coat from the quilt scraps, turn it roughly, and throw it to the ground in disgust. The others were just as particular. But Rhea kept her eye on the woman at the buggy who had not run at the porch with the others. Rhea passed the shotgun back to Mrs. Pepper.

"You bolted the back door?" Rhea asked Mrs. Pepper, and she nodded. "Stay back by the door, John Luke," said Rhea, as she walked past the busy women on the steps to the buggy. Rhea reached under the seat and pulled out the rifle, placing it casually in the crook of her arm as she reached back for the doctor's bag.

"Is there a doctor man in yonder with sick folks?" the woman with the sores asked.

154

"No," Rhea said. "He's gone to a neighbor's to get some help for the digging."

"Diggin'?"

"Yes. We've lost two to typhus," Rhea said. "When he comes back we're going to have to burn . . ."

But before Rhea could finish the woman beside the buggy was yelling. "Typhus! There's typhus in the house!" The other women drew back from the porch, throwing down Maude Pepper's quilt scraps and peas and feather sacks, wiping their dirty hands on their dirty rags.

"You should have cried it out to us!" the leader said. "Told us there was typhus here!" The corn women left us then, going back over the southern ridge toward the Arkansas River and Fort Smith, where they would get free passage on a train or boat further south. The last one took the quilt airing on Mrs. Pepper's clothesline.

"Why, Rhea," Maude Pepper said. "You're an awful liar!"

"And it comes so amazingly easy and natural to me," Rhea said. "Check the back, John Luke." I went off one end of the porch and Rhea around the other. We startled one of the ragged women who sat out back on the chopping block. She jumped up, dropping something on the ground. It was a fist-sized wad of paper money, some of it Yankee, money the "indigent" corn women begged off our good neighbors.

"My man made me do it," she said. "He said we'as pore, and youin' down here could spare it. He ain't feelin' like workin'. I ain't the only one a takin' money. They all got money. Some more than me."

"Your friends are gone," Rhea said. "Take your money and go after them." The ragged woman grabbed up the money and ran off after the others.

"Why, Rhea," I said. "Those women are out for gain."

Rhea laughed and shook her head. "It's part of the human condition. War brings out the best and the worst."

The worst of the human condition was soon to reveal itself to my child's mind. Crysop had spent most of the winter south of the Arkansas River. Now he was back, and we were soon to see his tracks on our land. He rode down on our neighbors with renewed vigor.

156

On a warm day, our yard filled with old sheets and clothes catching the wind like China clippers. While Rhea and Hillary washed clothes and hung them on the line to dry, Sarah and I were building a kite. Rhea carried a wicker basket full of dried clothes into the house, and returning checked our progress on the kite.

"Look," said Sarah, pointing toward a man walking into our yard. Walter England came leading his mule with Maude Pepper atop. It was plain to see that Mrs. Pepper was hurt, having trouble staying on the animal even with Mr. England's help. Rhea left us and went down the steps at a run. She and England got Mrs. Pepper to the porch and helped her down gently.

"Be careful of her hands, Mrs. Dameron," Walter England said, as he and Rhea helped her up the stairs.

"I got to sit a minute, rest, catch my breath," said Maude Pepper. They let her sit down on the top step. Rhea quickly sat beside her to look at the bloody broken hands Mrs. Pepper carried carefully against her body. There was no blood in the old woman's tear-streaked face. It had all drained away with the pain and shock.

"Bring the brandy and my bag," Rhea said to me and I split off to get them. When I returned, Hillary had already gotten a pan of warm water and lye soap and fresh towels. We all stood on the porch then, watching Rhea help Mrs. Pepper with the brandy. She drank the fiery liquid without batting an eye and waited for more.

"What happened, Mr. England?" Rhea asked, filling the cup again.

"I found her on the Van Buren Road. Sad to say, I thought she was drunk from the way she staggered about, but when I got near I saw her hands. She's not been too plain in telling what happened, but I believe raiders came to her place."

"Raiders! Damn 'em for thieves and scoundrels!" Maude Pepper said suddenly. "Rode into my little place and wanted my money, like I had money. 'Boys,' I said. 'I got no gold. I live by trading what I grow or make for what I need. In my whole life I never had fifty hard dollars in a piece.' But they didn't listen. They busted in my cabin—tore it apart and threw my few things into the yard. They even tried to pull the stones out of the fireplace."

Rhea gave Mrs. Pepper more brandy. She

drank deeply, and a more relaxed look began coming over her face. Then she recounted,

"'Catch her up,' the old man said. 'She'll tell us where the nigger's gold is when she feels the pain.'

"'What nigger's gold?' I said.

"'You sold a boy in Ft. Smith for gold,' the old buzzard said.

"'I never owned a black man, and I sure haven't been trading in slaves,' I said. But that truth was no never-mind to Crysop. He had one of his animals break my little finger.

"'Tell,' he said.

"'I can't,' I said. 'There's nothing I can tell you. I got no gold.' They broke more of my fingers but I couldn't give 'em no gold. Finally I screamed, 'I'd tell you, my God, I'd tell you if I had any gold. There's my dead husband's watch. That's as close to gold as I got and it's plated. It's in my trunk in the shed with his clothes.' Well, they went for that, perked right up, and got Bill's old watch.

"'Burn her out for lying,' Crysop said. 'This lesson will teach ye to stay clear of slavin'.'

"'I never owned slaves,' I said, and the boy of Crysop's pounded his rifle butt into my other hand and busted it. 'Liar,' he called me, and

159

rode out swinging my husband's watch. Every one of that sorry bunch of thieves took something, any little thing, when they left."

Mrs. Pepper was not hurting by the time she finished the brandy Rhea kept giving her. She lay back against the porch post and closed her eyes. "Thank God you found me, Walter England," she whispered. Rhea bathed the swollen broken hands, set the fingers one by one, and made a little paddle to hold each hand. Walter England carried Mrs. Pepper upstairs to bed. Maude Pepper stayed with us a few days, but she was of special concern to the Englands. In a few days they came and got her. They loved her and nursed her to full health. The salty little Mrs. Pepper and the Quaker family lived together from that time on. Walter England built her a small cabin on his place. And in time George England took over farming Maude Pepper's old homestead.

It was hard for me to understand Crysop's obsession with slavery, his unfair treatment of old Mrs. Pepper whom he said he suspected of selling a slave. I had seen few Negroes, knew none but Hillary, who seemed to me to do as she liked. But the area around Cane Hill had many slaves, property of the prosperous Cumberland Presbyterians who'd settled there.

The Presbyterian sect believed the Bible, and thus God, spoke for slavery, supported it by defining the duties of slave and master in Exodus 21. They also believed they were to teach the black man of Christ, in effect, to spread the gospel to him. In that way, though his body was in bondage in this world, his soul would be saved and free in the Kingdom, the only egalitarian reality.

I suppose, there were good masters and bad masters among the Presbyterians, but I had little firsthand knowledge, not seeing them regularly or, as it were, eating their portion. I had seen the thickly muscled black men who worked the coal seam at the Morrow place labor long and hard.

But hard work did not seem in itself bad to us because every man on the frontier who took the land by force from nature worked hard and long. Most did not think much of the right or wrong of owning another person. People were mostly busy with their crops and stock, with sick children, or with fuel for winter—everyday things. We did not see slavery as an unredeemable absolute wrong as we now know it was. It was just a fact in our world then, overlooked in its familiarity. We wanted to hold our own course and let the other man hold his with as few external pressures as possible. We were free men and took that pretty much at face value. We valued self-discipline and expected other men to do the same.

But of course human beings, being what they are, some men became corruptions, sores infecting the body and worse still the soul of mankind. I felt sad and ashamed when I tried to imagine people being sold and beaten and separated from their families. Yet slavery was no felt reality for me until Rhea and I called at the Dockery place.

Driving into the yard, I felt a heartsickness at the low and dejected cabins where Dockery's blacks lived. There were no windows in the log buildings and the door bar was on the outside, to keep the wretched human beings inside instead of danger out. A boy of fourteen or so was tied to the front porch by his neck, the rope wrapped around and around the post until only six inches of play remained in it. His hands were tied behind him. Dockery sat on the porch, tipped back in a cane bottomed chair.

Rhea was grim as she and I walked past the

boy up the step. She held me by the shoulder. Dockery did not stand up like a gentleman. He sat, still tipped back, tapping a whip handle on his leg, enjoying the boy's struggle to stay on his feet. "Run away," he said. "Lincoln's set him free." He laughed an ugly laugh. "But Jed Dockery ain't. Has he, boy?"

Rhea said nothing and shepherded me inside. The place was dark. Candles burned in the daytime. No windows here either, and the door bar was inside and stout to keep out any rebellious slaves. I saw a black girl cooking on the open hearth; another idly wiped the table and set it for lunch.

"Set two more places, Susie," a high-pitched voice said from a corner of the darkness. Mrs. Dockery was an invalid, confined to bed. Rhea did not doctor her regularly, but had been sent for that day. "Good to see you, Mrs. Dameron," the Dockery woman said.

"And you, Mrs. Dockery," Rhea replied. "Your message said your legs were troubling you." Rhea sat beside the bed.

"Who's the boy?" Mrs. Dockery asked, eyeing me suspiciously. "You ain't got no natural children, have you?"

"This is John Luke Pierce. He wants to be a

163

doctor one day," Rhea said, looking at me and smiling. She opened her bag.

"I don't want him around my bed," the woman said.

"Sit at the table," Rhea told me.

"Or in the cabin when you're treating me," Mrs. Dockery continued.

Rhea frowned. She didn't want me outside, and I didn't want to be there. "I'd rather he stayed in the house, Mrs. Dockery. He can sit quietly at the table."

"Don't want him around. Go to the porch, boy," the woman said.

"Mrs. Dockery, your husband is tormenting a Negro out there, I don't want my boy part of that," Rhea said.

"Too good, eh? You always was too good for plain folks, Rhea Dameron. 'My boy,' you calls him, but we that knows knows God punishes you by making you barren. You're not too good for that," said Mrs. Dockery.

"How can I help you, Mrs. Dockery?" Rhea said slowly and softly. "I must go soon."

"Set at the table, boy," the woman said to me. "My legs pain me terrible. My laudnum's gone. My neighbor said you had some for Sara Winters the other day." Rhea reached to pull back Mrs. Dockery's cover. The old woman slapped her hand so hard I heard it pop clear across the room. "Don't mess with me. I know what I need. I been in this bed for years, and I'm the judge of what comforts me."

"I can't give you anything without examining you. Mrs. Dockery, It might be just the wrong thing, then I'd be guilty of causing you more pain," Rhea explained.

"Nonsense," Mrs. Dockery said, looking at Rhea's face, testing it for indecision or opportunity. "I'll take the responsibility for it."

"I can't allow you to take my responsibility," Rhea said unmoved.

Mrs. Dockery threw back the covers from her legs then. "Look your eyes out," she said.

Rhea examined the legs. "You must want laudnum very badly," she laid. "How long have you been without it?"

"Three days. The old man 'forgot it' in Ft. Smith and wouldn't go back till he caught that boy. Those nigger girls yonder rob me of it whenever I go to sleep. They giggle behind my back like I don't know. But I know what goes on around here. I know!" Mrs. Dockery almost shouted. The black girls looked at each other and smiled at the old woman's impotent anger.

Rhea pulled the cover back over Mrs. Dockery's legs. "You've taken laudnum a long time, haven't you?"

"Only thing that helps the pain," the frail woman said, almost crying.

"Mrs. Dockery, rubbing your legs, soaking them in warm water and epsom salts would be better for you. Using the muscles a little each day would restore strength, and you could regain some movement, get about the house and yard."

"I don't want to get about this place," the woman hissed. "You're your father all over again. Give me my medicine or get."

"I'll give you what I can spare," Rhea said, and gave Mrs. Dockery a small bottle.

The Dockery woman grabbed it. "Why it ain't full. Not one day's worth."

Rhea stood up. "It's against my judgment to give you that. I do hope it helps you until Mr. Dockery gets more." Mrs. Dockery didn't hear Rhea. She was too busy with her medicine.

We went back to the porch. Rhea held me in the door a long moment watching Dockery and the Negro boy. "Give me your knife," she said. I opened it and handed it to her. Rhea Dameron took it and began to cut through the rope.

166

Dockery jumped up, dropping his chair to the porch.

"That's a new rope," he said. Rhea kept cutting. "You've no right to interfere with my property."

"And you've no right to interfere with my peace of mind. As long as I'm here and I see what I believe to be wrong, I have to do something about it." Dockery seemed to draw back the whip. "Do you propose to beat me, sir?" Rhea said looking him straight in the eye. She stood up in his face. "If so, do it. There are laws to deal with you on that."

He backed off, and Rhea pulled the cut rope loose from the boy's neck. Dockery picked up his chair and sat down while I fetched water. Rhea washed the wounds and talked quietly to the boy. When she'd finished her work she turned to Dockery. "Even an animal does better with kindness and encouragement," she said.

"Niggers ain't got the sense of an animal," Dockery said, spitting contemptuously.

"That must be because they are human beings like the rest of us," Rhea said. "You owe me twenty dollars, Mr. Dockery." That was the first time I ever heard Rhea ask for a fee and such a high fee it was.

167

"The hell you say," he snorted.

"Pay up or I shall be forced to take back your wife's medicine," Rhea said. Dockery grudgingly reached into his pocket and pulled forth a long wallet. Rhea accepted a gold coin. We left the Dockery place then.

Rhea drove briskly, fuming and silent, holding the gold coin in her hand with the reins. Her anger had not cooled by the time we reached Cane Hill. We drove up to Judge Woodward's. The old man, clad in a once fine broadcloth suit, was in his yard examining the azalea bushes along the side of his neat white house. Rhea wrapped the reins and went to him.

"Good day, Rhea," the judge said over his picket fence.

Rhea barely nodded. "Judge, I've just come from that trash Dockery's place. He's been abusing a Negro boy. I believe he's holding other blacks in their cabins." She paused to breathe.

"No, Rhea," the judge said. "There are just a couple of young girls and the boy left. Dockery sold the rest further south ten days ago."

168

"He can't do that," she said. "Lincoln. The Union troops here."

"He did, child."

Rhea handed the coin she still held to the judge. "I took this," she said. "It's for the boy. I know you'll see he gets it."

"I'll put it aside," the judge said, going toward his steps. "For King James Dockery slave and son of Jed Dockery." He went inside to write down in his careful record the money and the name.

Rhea and I went home to Lord's Vineyard and the peace it held against the world of men like Dockery, who victimize the bodies of some and the minds and souls of the rest.

10

THE peace at Lord's Vineyard was drawing to an end for Rhea and for me, and the next days were to test her and compel me to question her very character. It began about a week after the trip to the Dockery place. I looked up from my wood chopping and saw smoke coming from beyond the south mountain.

"Rhea, look," I said, running in the back door. She stepped to the porch and watched the smoke.

"It's Huggins' place," she said. "Hillary, Claudia, get the chickens." Rhea and I drove the horse and our five sheep to the manger cave, and left Sarah and Hillary and Claudia trying to catch a few of the hens to hide away. We walked fast as we could through the hills toward the smoke. By the time we got there, Huggins' barn was gone, and the house was starting to fall in. His dogs lay dead in the yard. The old man lay there, too, stretched out faceup with a bloody hole through his middle.

170

Rhea knelt beside him. She stroked his wide forehead, smoothing the balding hairline. Huggins opened his eyes. "Rhea, there ain't no sense to it. I give 'em what I had, give it to 'em. Crysop. They shot my dogs. They killed us for the pure pleasure of it." Then Huggins was gone. Rhea and I had another grave to dig.

By the time Rhea and I got home, it was getting late. The farm looked normal as we came over the hill, except there were not but two chickens in the yard. Hillary and Claudia were taking down the laundry from the line beside the kitchen. There was a bearded man sitting on his horse talking to Claudia. Two of our hams hung from his saddle, and the smokehouse door stood open. Ed Huggins' old smoothbore rifle with its Indian-beaded sheath was stuck in his bedroll. He was sitting loose in the saddle, resting his weight on one leg with the other out of the stirrup draped across the seat as he watched Claudia.

"Do you see any more, John Luke?" Rhea asked.

"No, ma'am," I said. "I believe he's by himself."

"So do I," Rhea said. "He's separated from the rest for some reason. Scout maybe. Maybe they were in a hurry to get to a saloon." We were already halfway down to the clothes line as she talked.

The rider sized up Rhea. "Why here's us another one. Ain't as purty as this 'un, but you'll do. Yesiree, you'll do just fine. The boys'll be proud I made this here little side trip."

Rhea didn't say anything, she just reached up like she was going to take down my Sunday shirt from the line. Instead, she pulled the line down tight and let it fly up in the rider's face. She jabbed the horse's flank with a piece of stove wood she'd picked up passing the wood-pile. The animal reared and dropped its bearded rider hard against our stone porch steps. The next I knew Rhea was yelling, "John Luke, get the horse!" Hillary and I caught the horse. When I looked back Rhea was kneeling on the steps near the raider's chest, the stove wood was raised to strike. But as I watched, she slowly lowered it. It was plain the man was dead. His head sat at a funny angle on his shoulders. He'd broken his neck in the fall.

The three women and I loaded the body on his horse. Rhea and I took it back toward Ed Huggins' place. About a mile south of there, we dumped it off a bluff into the river. Rhea had stripped him of his guns and ammunition at the house. At the river she threw his saddle and bridle into the water and turned the horse loose. It was night when we returned home. When we came inside Hillary and Claudia and Sarah were sitting at the table before their full untouched plates. Rhea washed her hands and sat down. For a long time the women didn't say anything. They picked at their food, but never got the forks to their mouths.

"Why'd you kill him?" Claudia asked Rhea.

"If he'd gotten to Crysop by tomorrow morning, you wouldn't be able to ask," Rhea said.

"It was senseless, senseless. He was just passing the time of day."

"It *was* senseless. Lately a lot of things seem pretty senseless to me. We are going to have to be careful now. Part of the animals must always be hidden. We must keep only a little meat and food where the raiders can find it," Rhea said.

"You killed that man for passing the time of day with me," Claudia said.

"Claudia, you cannot flirt and tease men like that. They are not boys and they will not play your coquette game. They are savages. My God,

173

we had just buried Edd Huggins. He and his friends killed that old man for sport. He had Edd's gun on his saddle.

"You never gave him a chance," Claudia said.

After the raider's death, Rhea left every night. She was home each morning to help with the work as usual. Our household now took on a new alertness for any intruders, and I spent many hours sitting on the mountains watching for any riders. Claudia did not speak to Rhea or Hillary. She kept to herself in her room, taking her meals there on a tray. Rhea worked the two gardens, tended the vineyard and orchard, and nursed the sick who came or sent word to Vineyard.

Walter England plowed for us and did our planting that spring. He was a good neighbor now. But still, Rhea carried the load. She was silent—maybe from tiredness, maybe because she had things on her mind like killing the raider. She didn't talk about whatever it was. I asked her once why she worked so hard. She said it needed doing, it kept her mind busy, and she said one day Jamie Dameron was coming home and Vineyard would be there. Hillary, I noticed, began to watch her closely, seeing the tensions building, unable to stop them. Finally Claudia brought matters to a head.

One afternoon, she joined us for lunch. Her auburn hair was neatly arranged. She was wearing a grey dress in place of the black we had become accustomed to.

"I would like to move into town as soon as possible, Rhea," Claudia said. "I believe I should like it better there. I do not wish to be here any longer. I shall take a place in town, find a nurse for Joey, and join with other genteel ladies in caring for the sick and wounded, making bandages and clothing."

"You've never shown any interest in the sick here," Rhea said.

"And you've never considered my feelings or my needs," answered Claudia.

"What need, Claudia?" Rhea asked.

"My need for a wet nurse, for one thing. How am I to recover from my grief when I am daily reminded of my dead husband by his nursing child? I asked you for the nurse he promised in December, and you have done nothing. You solve every problem but mine."

Rhea put her hand on her forehead. "Claudia, you cannot live alone in town with a

175

baby. There are too many wild men about. You'd be their prey."

"At the quilting party, Martha Pain said that there are many fine eligible young men. Young men from good families, wealthy families up North away from this war."

"And what will these eligible young men think of Joey?" Rhea asked.

"Why in time, after they know me, they would accept my baby."

"Claudia, if I get you a cow or something will you stay on the farm, at least leave Joey here?" Rhea asked.

"I would consider that," Claudia said. "For a while."

Next morning Rhea and I set off for Blackie Foard's place. Foard kept goats. Rhea planned to buy a nanny and kid. If Foard wasn't there, his woman and the goats would be. We wound through the hills and valleys all that fine spring morning until we came to the creek that ran through Foard's homestead. Before we reached the water two quick shots banged into the shimmering surface, throwing up little fountains in front of us.

"Far enough," a man's voice said. "Who be you?"

"Rhea Dameron, Foard. I come on business. I want to buy a milk goat."

"Come ahead, then," the hidden voice said.

By the time we reached the cabin, Foard had put an arm through his suspenders and was waiting for us. His woman, the siren of the hills, according to Gilstrap and the Grahams, came to the door. She was a little fuzzy haired woman, well past young and mighty dry-looking. Her skin was freckled and blotchy and her stomach stuck out noticeably under her dirty apron.

"Get down and set," Foard said amiably. "It's a pure pleasure seein' you again, Missus Dameron. That's there's my missus."

Rhea nodded to Mrs. Foard as Blackie offered a black grimy hand to Rhea. "Nice place you got here, Mr. Foard. Lots of good water it looks like."

I tried to see the nice place Rhea saw, but I only saw buckets and cans thrown about the yard. The cabin's porch roof had collapsed at one end from rot. A wagon in pieces was drawn up under a tree where tools and grease buckets and rags littered the ground. On top of this a number of scrawny goats nibbled at every edible on the place. I suspected they even waited beside rocks for a green shoot to push its way up.

"I've let her go some since my brother's untimely death," Foard said.

"I'd heard he was killed," Rhea said. "I'm sorry. I hoped the matter between you and the Grahams could be settled without killing."

"I ain't going to get 'em back, if that's worrying you, Missus Dameron. I figure there's a higher law to deal with killers. Seen it come to pass just yesterday."

"How's that?" Rhea asked walking toward a nanny that looked a little less scrawny than the others. She offered her hand to the aromatic creature who sniffed her fingertips.

"Somebody killed two of Crysop's gang."

"Really?" Rhea said, watching the goat.

"Yeah, caught 'em on the road drunk and drew down on 'em. Bullet right through one's heart; the other's forehead. Federal boys found a minie ball by each of their bodies."

"Minie ball?" I said.

"That's right, youngin'. A minie ball for the conscripts, like the ones they didn't fire at the Yanks at Prairie Grove. That's three of Crysop's

178

boys gone—one disappeared, two killed. But that's makin' the old bird kinda edgy."

I looked at Rhea. She met my eyes steadily and asked, "What do you want for this goat, Mr. Foard?"

"Oh, that un's a good un," he said. "She's fresh and got a good big kid, too."

"I'll buy them both if your price is reasonable," Rhea said.

"Now, Missus Dameron, you didn't drive all the way our here to go home empty-handed. You're planning to pay my price," Foard said.

I could see the bargaining was on so I went off toward the wagon under the tree. Foard had a lot of tools, good solid workman's tools. I tried a ball peen hammer against the iron rim creating a ring. His spoke plane lay in a pile of curly shavings. I picked up a couple of the curls and tried to straighten them out. They were dry and broke.

"Fetch me some twine off that wagon!" Foard shouted. I picked up the small short ropes I saw and started back. Foard trussed up the nanny and kid and threw 'em up on Rhea's buggy boot. "There go, ma'am," he said. "You got yourself a fine pair of critters there. And I know they'll have a fine home, too."

Rhea stood considering the animals, pitiful and resentful of their bound state. She bent closer to consider a spot on the mother's skin. "John Luke, will you fetch the money pouch out of my bag."

I climbed into the buggy and opened the leather bag of bottles, bandages, and instruments. A soft deerskin pouch held Rhea's coins. I found it quickly. But it was not the coin purse. Instead the pouch I opened contained five shining minie balls—one for each of the remaining Crysop gang and one for the informer. I closed the pouch and looked again for the coin bag. It had fallen on the floor. As I picked it up my hand brushed the cold steel of a .36 caliber Navy Colt. There were two of the pistols and a Sharps rifle under the rug. All were loaded and primed.

"Hurry up, John Luke," Rhea said. I closed the pouch and put it back in the bag.

11

"YOU killed those Crysop men," I said as we drove back toward Vineyard through the spring afternoon. "You did it in cold blood. You're a no-good hypocrite."

Rhea Dameron drove on holding the reins loosely, looking straight ahead. She didn't say anything for a long time. At last she said, "John Luke, you are most probably right."

I didn't like Rhea after that. I shunned her company. I quit going to the infirmary and to Sunday worship. I was disgusted that she, a professing believer and healer, had killed two men—three if you counted the raider who died at Lord's Vineyard. She may not have actually done that killing, but as I looked back, it was plain she had meant to with that stick of wood. I began to see her faults, the other sinister side of every action. She had drawn down on that old man at the graveyard in Prairie Grove when we buried Doctor Isaacs and my pa. She'd interfered in the fight between Blackie Foard and

Gilstrap in Fayetteville. She'd tried to tell the Yankee captain how to run his business. Bitter as it was to take, my pa was in the Confederate service, and Crysop had performed a soldier's duty in attacking the cave. How was I or anybody else ever to know what happened in the cave? It was war, and war was different from other times. Maybe Crysop had to kill those men. We only had Rhea's word he'd been there anyway. Maybe he hadn't been there at all. Maybe Rhea just wanted her competition out of the way.

I began to see Rhea's nighttime trips differently, too. Maybe they were not for good or mercy. There were other killings—lots of folks died mysteriously in those days. Marauders always got the blame, but who was to say that the marauder was not one above-suspicion woman. And there was that manger cave stocked full of plunder, more than she could grow or buy. Maybe Rhea Dameron was nothing but a plain thief, marauding the countryside like the other wolves, only smarter and deadlier because she was a woman and unsuspected.

I doubted every action and motive of the woman who had been my friend. I was as blind to her virtues as I had been to her faults. The change was complete, total. It did not go unnoticed.

Rhea struggled with the broken plow, trying to get the heavy awkward tool on the wagon. I just stood against the kitchen porch rail watching her, not offering to help.

"You there you took root so deep you can't help out around here?" Hillary asked behind me. "Get out there and lend a hand, boy."

I went on watching, not offering to move. "Don't reckon I will," I said. "I ain't Rhea Dameron's slave like you are."

Hillary came down the stairs and took me by the shoulders. "Who are you calling a slave, white boy? Me. Well, you're wrong, boy. I'm a free woman. Abe Lincoln didn't set me free January first this year. Doctor Isaacs set me free ten years ago. I have been a free woman since the doctor brought me to his house and healed me up from the whip. I'm free as you. Free to choose. And I choose to stay around good people. I know bad times, boy. Bad times is bad people. I ran away four times to get my baby back, and four times I was dragged back and beaten by my baby's white father. Last time he rubbed salt in the wounds. Doctor

183

Isaacs brought me and my baby away from that. I got a place here, boy, because I want it. Right here I can do a whole lot of good and help a lot of people with the skills I've learned."

"If you're free how come you didn't have to leave when the other freemen did before the war? That was a law," I said.

"My son did. But I didn't have any better place to go. I wanted to stay here. It's my home. The Isaacs and Damerons helped me stay, kept quiet, and let folks think I still belonged to them. All the time my freedom papers were in my trunk."

"They lied for you and broke the law," I said. "Rhea Dameron's a liar. I know enough on her to get her hung anytime in Fayetteville. You're a plain fool sucking up to her, believing she's good." I said.

"Wait one minute. Back up. What's this garbage about getting her hung?" Hillary asked me.

"It's plain fact Rhea Dameron killed that raider here. She killed two more outside Fayetteville. Shot one in the heart; one in the forehead. She did it from ambush, in cold blood, or she couldn't have done it at all," I said, glad to have my secret out.

184

"Little boy, she can shoot the eyes out of a snake at three hundred yards. If she's a bloody killer, and you know it, how come you're still alive. You've thought it all out but that, haven't you?" Hillary said.

"She'd be scared to kill me, living in her own house and all. Folks would get suspicious."

"Boys die all the time—falling, drowning, diseases. If she wanted to kill you, you'd be dead. Don't you think it's strange she hasn't killed you, you being able to get her hung anytime. She must be crazy or mighty good," said Hillary.

"She ain't crazy," I said. "And she ain't good. She's a cold-blooded killer."

"You want to know about those Crysop men, boy? You go there where they died and walk out in the woods. You'll find you a little bitty grave—a baby grave, a baby who never got a chance to live his life because two drunken men couldn't leave a sixteen-year-old pregnant refugee girl alone. Rhea came on that, and she killed them both because they didn't think about anything but their lust. She helped the girl and buried what was her baby. Now she didn't make any show or claim about her actions because the girl had been through her share already," Hillary said.

"She say!" I said. "How come she had those minie balls to put by their heads? How come she's got a pouch with five more, waiting for the rest of the Crysop men who were at the cave?"

"She picked up those minie balls at Prairie Grove beside her brother's body. She's had them with her ever since, a reminder. She put them there to identify those men as the Eden's Bluff killers." Hillary sat down on the step then. "Maybe she put them there to scare up that bunch of snakes."

Spring comes in spells in the mountains, easing us warily into the time of true warmth that lasts until late fall. March is a bitter month of icy wind and late storms. April dallies with the mind and heart, offering the hope of bright spring days with one hand and dashing it with cold rainy weeks with the other. By May there is more true warmth than cold, and life settles into an expectation of vegetation and growth as coats find their way into the closet for good. My own period of love and hate for Rhea Dameron paralleled the season of nature's changeable youth. My true warmth came in late spring.

Rhea and I were not friends since I found the minie balls. Hillary's explanation had made me think, but I was too proud to admit I might be wrong. The way I looked at it then, if I'd been certain Rhea was good, and then, just as certain she was bad, and I changed yet again to a certainty, my judgment was suspect. I was just a weathervane, changing with every breeze, without a mind or direction of my own. No one would trust me, least of all me. Pa said a man had to stand for something. But he never said what, and he was not around long enough for me to develop any refined understanding of what a man should be. Yet I knew I had to hold on somewhere or drown in a sea of opinions. I had lost my surety. I could not admit that. I never admitted I was wrong about Rhea, never said I was sorry. I couldn't. Not yet, not out loud. But I began to watch again—to look for a balance to weigh things. I no longer shunned her company, but I was silent and watched.

In early May, Rhea, Hillary, and I went to the Adler's place to deliver their daughter's child. Like mant young women, Sally had been caught in the romance of war and the marriage epidemic that brought many to bed with child, although the husband had long since returned to army life. Mrs. Adler herself was a trifle light on brains, given to spending whole days in the yard in her chemise playing the piano, which she did admirably. Only she and a simple-minded boy named Toby were at home when Sally's time came. Adler himself had come for us, then gone after Mrs. Adler's cousin. Hillary and I went with Rhea to help with things.

Hillary's job was to keep Mrs. Adler under control and to prepare food. My job was to cut wood and help around the place with chores and such. The baby was slow coming. I caught up with chores. After a lunch of red beans, corn bread, and greens, I went out into the sunlight. The sun and smell of growing things gave me a great contentment. I lazily climbed into an old tree, surveyed the peaceful view before me. I saw Hillary go to the creek for water, but decided not to tag along since she had not called me. I'd learned there were times I was not welcome and decided, women being the way they were, this might be one. I guess I fell asleep.

By the time I heard the men, they were already in the yard. There were five of them, and they had two Negro girls up behind them on their horses. I recognized the girls from that trip to the Dockery place. From the looks of the men and the booty hanging from their saddles, they were trouble. They had come out of nowhere, randomly following their blood trail over the hills toward town. Rhea was alone in the house with a crazy woman and boy and a girl giving birth.

"See who's inside," the leader ordered.

A rider dismounted and started for the door. But Rhea met him and backed him up. She was drying her hands, and I could see she was spitting mad.

"What do you want here?" she asked.

The young man who was the leader swept off his hat. "Whatever you have to offer a poor bunch of soldiers, ma'am."

"You are not a poor bunch of soldiers," Rhea said. "You're plain thieves, and we have nothing to give you here. You might leave us one of those hams on your saddle." Old Mrs. Adler came to the door.

"Hurry, Missy," she said. Rhea turned to go.

"Wait a minute," the man said. "Have you contraband in this house?"

"We have nothing in this house, but a baby

189

trying to be born," Rhea said. Sally cried out from inside, and Rhea moved toward the door.

"I have a report of contraband on this farm."

"You have a report as false as your heart," Rhea said, and started inside.

"Stop her," the leader said. The man on the porch put his arm across the doorway and grinned. "Bob, Garret, check the house." The men quickly dismounted and went inside. Two minutes later they were back.

"Will, there ain't nothing in there but a pregnant girl hollering and an old woman crying and wringing her hands."

One of the Negro girls slipped off the horse behind the raider and giggled and flashed her way onto the porch. She seemed different from the first time I saw her. She swayed when she walked, and the men followed her hungrily with their eyes. They laughed when she stumbled. She smiled at the laughs, but she was not as drunk as she pretended, not as drunk as the men. When she stood before Rhea she reached out and felt the material of Rhea's sleeve.

"Nice," she said. "Very nice. Guess you a lady," she said, circling Rhea. "A lady what keeps a nigger gal to do her work. Why ain't you Missus Dameron, what come to help old lady Dockery? Why, yes, you's Missus Dameron. You got a nice farm, a rich husband off fighting, a kind heart for *poor Negroes*, and a nigger girl of your own fetchin' for you at a birthin'. Where's your nigger, Missus Dameron?" She poked Rhea in the stomach with her finger. Rhea's hand closed over the woman's fist and held it.

"I'm right here," Hillary said from the side of the porch. She didn't have the water pails. She was standing straight and proud. "But I am not a nigger, girl. I'm black a you, but I'm no nigger. Nobody ever made me feel like a nigger till you rode in here with that white trash. You are an embarrassment. What do you want with decent people anyway?"

"I had enough decent people," the girl said. "I ain't no fine house nigger wif uppity ideas, but I been chased around the barn by decent people enough. They ain't no different'n the rest of us. Not old man Dockery. Not Doc Isaacs. He kept you for more than housework, gal. I ain't no fool, and you don't need to put on airs with us knowing folks. You crazy taking up for this white woman. She may talk nice and act nice to us, but she bleeds white blood. Like

191

they say, blood is thicker than anything." Just then Sally screamed out in the house.

"Get out of my way," Rhea said, and started for the door.

I saw a flash and a red stain started to grow across the stomach of Rhea's white shirt. The next I knew the man by the door had the black girl, and she was screaming filthy words as he hauled her down the porch. She broke free and ran back toward Rhea, waving a fancy straight razor over her head.

"You can't doctor Missus Dockery no more. Won't do her no good. I done surgery on her myself this morning. I 'spect I killed that old white bitch," she said. "I'm hungry for blood, warm white woman's blood." She swung the razor again, and Rhea dodged. The black girl tested her with feints and thrusts, but each time Rhea evaded them by stepping away. The men on the horses laughed, watching the duel. One of the men on the porch held Hillary. Finally Rhea didn't have anywhere to go. The black girl smiled as she sought the kill.

"I waited a long time in that old dark cabin for this day when I gets my revenge," she said.

"She never hurt you!" Hillary yelled.

"She don't have to. She the wrong color today," the black girl said. "Today my turn."

Rhea watched the slashing razor, caught it as it came down, and stepped through the swing, pushing the girl's head against the wall. Then Rhea had the razor. She folded it up and put it in her skirt band. She caught the dazed girl and pushed her at the raider.

"Get out of here," she said to the raider. "There's nothing left to steal. And hate's a sickness I can't deal with."

The black girl reached up suddenly and ripped the gold hoops from Rhea's pierced ears. "Nothing left for sure now," she said. Blood ran down on Rhea's neck and collar, but she did not show any emotion.

"Close the door and burn the place," the leader said. The two dismounted men went inside. I saw brands from the hearth in their hands. They set fire to the curtains and bed ticking.

"There are people in there!" Rhea said.

"Did you see any people in there?" the leader, Will asked one of the others.

"No. No people, just Arky trash that ain't got nothing worth takin'. We always enjoys a fire when we don't get our pay," the raider said.

The firesetters dragged a featherbed out and set it against the door and fired it. It leaped into flame. Mrs. Adler's face was at the window.

"Damn you!" Rhea said to the raiders. "Damn you all to hell!"

"Get 'em out, brave lady," the leader said and laughed. "If you can."

Rhea and Hillary sped to the door, kicked and dragged the mattress away, and opened the flaming door. I saw Rhea grab Mrs. Adler as she ran across the room. She handed the woman to Hillary, who took her away from the porch toward my tree. The old woman was shaking and crying. Rhea went back inside. She stayed a long time. We heard her calling Toby Adler's name above the roaring flames. Sometimes we could hear him singing. Finally Rhea came out the side door, half-dragging, half-carrying Sally. Hillary and I, holding tight on Mrs. Adler, went to help. We got Sally under a tree and covered her with the bed quilt Rhea brought her in. Rhea stood up and started back, but the house was caving in. I went with her to the side window; the curtains were burning, but we could see Toby singing amidst the flames. Rhea kept calling him, "Over here, Toby! Toby, come this way!" She was halfway in the

194

window, reaching out for him as he stood across the room watching the fire falling around him.

"Bring me that log over here," Rhea said to me, pointing at a fat old piece of trunk by the woodpile. She tore out the curtains while I got it. She climbed up and boosted herself into the window. It looked as though Toby was coming to her. He walked toward the window, but then he just sat down in the flames, and before Rhea could get him the floor collapsed. After that we didn't hear Toby Adler singing anymore. Rhea came out and sat on the stump. She was covered with soot and her own blood. She was crying.

The raider leader rode his horse almost up on the stump, so close Rhea had to stand up. He looked in the window and down at Rhea. "Too bad," he said. "You're quite a fire-eater. Be seeing you, ma'am." He reached down then and caught Hillary about the waist and lifted her to the saddle. "This Confederate contraband has to be deposited at the Rhea's Mill holding camp. They're moving 'em to Kansas first of the week."

Rhea grabbed for the bridle. "She's not contraband. She's a free woman." Hillary squirmed to get loose, but he held on. "Your papers, Hillary," Rhea said. "Where are your papers?"

"At home, my papers are at home," Hillary answered.

"If you got papers on this nigger wench bring 'em to Rhea's Mill tomorrow," the raider said, and started to ride off. But Rhea still held the bit, and Hillary kept kicking.

"She's a free woman and should not be incarcerated in that pit." The raider struggled with Hillary and the horse, but did not respond to Rhea. I saw the desperation on Rhea's face. The holding camp was a hell hole, a place where blood lust and sexual violence went unchecked among the blacks and Union soldiers. "She's the property of a Union soldier and by law not subject to confiscation!" Rhea shouted at the raider. "My husband is Captain Jamie Dameron, and I can prove that." Rhea pulled a crumpled letter from her pocket and thrust it at the man fighting the frantic horse and Hillary. He seemed to look at the envelope, then dropped Hillary.

"Hell," he said. "This just ain't worth the trouble." He rode off on that fine spring day through the smoke and across the hill toward

Van Buren. My mouth tasted of smoke and hate.

Hillary ran toward Sally. She called Rhea to come. Rhea worked over the girl a long time. In the end, she saved the baby, but Sally died. Later that afternoon, Mr. Adler showed up with Mrs. Frieden, Mrs. Adler's cousin, and her son. Young Frieden had lost an arm in the war and seemed weak, still, but he took charge. He and Mr. Adler buried the dead. They loaded Mrs. Adler and the new baby on their wagon to take them home. His wife, Frieden said, would take the baby.

"It was God's will," Mrs. Frieden said from the box. "The will of God, Rhea."

"It was the will of Sweet William Crysop," Rhea said. That was the first I knew the raider was Crysop's son and that the brutal men belonged to Crysop's gang. But what I had seen was only the beginning.

12

I WOKE up one bright June morning with a problem on my mind. Sarah's birthday was coming, and since I was now the man of my family, I wanted to buy her a present, a store-bought present with money I had earned. The problem was I had no money and no way of making any. Grown men were hard pressed for money in that time, let alone a boy almost eleven. Rhea was in the orchard. I could see her wide-brimmed straw hat moving down among the trees. Each tree at Vineyard had a hive, tidy little patented gums as we called them then to mark them from the natural bee gums we cut down as sections of hollow tree. The man-made hives were part of Jamie Dameron's husbandry, brought from back East and Europe. But the bees belonged to Rhea. She had an affinity for the fuzzy little insects that stung other people.

"Rhea," I said. "I got to earn some money."

She sat down on the stone wall. "I suppose you are old enough and skilled enough to be paid for some work around here. Save us hiring a man, if we could find one."

"No," I said. "You payin' me would be just the same as giving me the money."

Rhea looked out across the valley. "Jamie used to plant that field in buckwheat just for the bees. He and I used to course bees in June until we had our hives set." I thought of Jamie Dameron's picture sitting on Rhea's dresser. His hair was slicked down some and he looked serious. Here was another side of the man. He had a little poem about bees:

> A swarm of bees in May
> Is worth a load of hay.
> A swarm of bees in June
> Is worth a silver spoon.
> A swarm of bees in July
> Is not worth a fly.

"It's June, isn't it?" Rhea said. "If you want to make money, find a honey run. You can get the bees and honey and wax yourself, or you can sell the run to someone who will."

"I don't like bees," I said.

"Neither did I, at first. But they are really

very pleasant little creatures once you know them," she said.

"I don't know anything about how to do bees," I said.

"I'll teach you," she said. "Then when I'm gone you can have my bees."

"Where are you going?"

"Nowhere," Rhea said. "But when a person that the bees know dies, somebody has to tell the bees, promise to do them good and take them over, or they perish."

"Is that a story?" I asked.

"Probably. But it's also an old custom. It sort of makes bees part of the family."

"They're bad to sting for family," I said.

"Not at all," Rhea said. "If you are kind with bees, they won't hurt you. Be brutal and so will they. If they sting you, they die. That's a high price for a temper fit so they won't sting unless what they care for is threatened. Then, they'll die to save it—same as people."

I thought about what she said, considered the bee's point of view. But I could not reconcile myself to the burning sting and welt it left. "I don't like being stung," I said.

"Well, John Luke, to get life's honey you must sometimes risk a few stings. Of course, if you were not serious about the money, I can understand. Maybe this isn't the year," Rhea said genuinely. She was always for letting you grow into things in your season.

"I reckon I can take a sting as well as the next," I said. "I aim to make me some money. And I truly like the taste of honey on biscuits, too. Why we can make candles out of the wax and mix up some cough medicine, too. Sell them, too."

"I hope it's a big hive—big as your plans," Rhea grinned.

"Why there isn't any limit to what can be done with a bee," I said. "Did you ever see a bee sitting around? Why they just live to work. The bee business could be very profitable. I might find hundreds of hives. I'm eager to learn about this bee business. Where do we start?"

"First, we must find a bee," Rhea said. I looked around. The orchard was full of bees. Some were even crawling on Rhea's hat. She read my thoughts. "A foreign bee. All these bees live here. We must go where there is a flowering field or water, find a bee, and course her back to the hive. I think I know the place to start. You get a smoker and bucket from the shed. I'll tell Hillary where we are going."

Edd Huggins' old place had a good field of clover. Bees purely loved the fat white blossoms. It wasn't hard to find a bee, but following a loaded bee can be hard because they spiral up and circle before they take off for the hive. They are easy to lose in the sun and against the trees.

Rhea said we could time a bee—sprinkle one with powder and see how long it took to come back, and get its distance, then narrow the direction down and find the hive. But she said that wasn't much sport, and she wasn't sure some bees didn't fly faster and maybe some stopped off for a drink. We decided to hold powder and timing for last-ditch efforts.

After several tries, we picked a bee and set out on the honey run. I ran to keep up with our little guide. Rhea laughed as I fell over logs and rocks, not daring to take my eye off the minute insect in the lush and verdant universe. We chased the bee for almost a mile south of Huggins' place, double teaming the creature, both trying to keep her in sight lest the other lose sight. We became caught up in our hunt and forgot the war in the beauty of the day and the country.

"She'll come down soon, John Luke," Rhea

said. "Watch close. They can go in a wood-pecker's hole or a knothole or crawl in on the ground. They can hive in fallen trees or logs or even rocks."

"There!" I yelled. "There she goes to that dead tree." I raced toward the tree fast as the bee herself. When she landed I felt victorious. But Rhea had stopped. She looked around, trying to get her bearings in the woods.

"I believe we've run onto Ned Frolley's land," she said. "Let's go back. Mark the hive if you want, but let's go. We'll leave word in town you found the hive and get his permission to take the honey."

"Aw, Rhea," I protested. "We found the tree. We've got our smoker and bucket."

"It's Frolley's tree. He's a whiskey-maker, boy. He does not want uninvited company. Come on," Rhea said.

I scribbled my mark on the trunk. I looked up at that lovely old dead tree full of sweetness as Rhea started back. I could taste the honey, imagine it on my biscuits at supper. Sarah's birthday money floated away before my eyes.

"Come on," Rhea said again. I ran to catch up.

"Dash it!" I said. "God made honey for

whoever finds it. It's as much Edd Huggins' for the clover as it is Ned Frolley's for the tree. And it's mine for the finding."

"That may be. But I'm not in a mood to get shot for a pot of honey when we've got plenty at home," she said, and kept walking along the ravine that ran along the hill.

"That's your honey! Couldn't we ask Frolley and go shares?" I asked.

"The danger's in going to ask."

"We could just take it then," I said.

"That's not right, boy. You must ask first. Too many take without asking now. You ask first. It's yours, but you must ask. And you must accommodate. You don't cut down any trees in this yard or a witness tree ever," she said.

"I don't want to cut for a hive. I didn't bring an axe or saw. I just want the honey," I said.

Rhea stopped. "You are set on that honey, aren't you?"

"Yes, ma'am. I'm set," I said. "Let's smoke the tree first, then go see Frolley."

"We'll see Frolley first," Rhea said looking sternly at me. Then she smiled. "If we're killed, at least, we can save the stings and work."

Frolley's house was south of the tree, close

to the Van Buren Road, so we angled across country. At first, I was pleased at my persuasion of Rhea Dameron. But as we walked, I began to think about what we were doing. Moonshiners were touchy about intruders. They didn't care much who got killed. Killing was just part of their business. They didn't bat an eye at killing. It made me edgy thinking about what could happen.

"Rhea, haven't you ever saved Frolley's life or his only precious child?" I asked.

"Frolley doesn't owe me any favors. If he did, I doubt it would matter out here," she said. "I sure hope we don't walk up on his still before we find the house."

Just then we topped a little ridge. Right below us sat Frolley's still, a wagon load of corn, and three of the meanest-looking men I'd ever seen. Rhea caught me just before I stumbled into plain sight. She held me with her hand over my mouth. In a little while her hand slipped away. "Which one's Frolley?" I asked.

"The one with his foot on the wheel hub," she said. Frolley was what we called a black man, although he was white by race. He had a heavy black beard and black hair bristled on his head. As another man shoveled the corn out of

205

the wagon onto a canvas tarp, he reached into his wide leather belt and held out a little bag to the man on the wagon box.

"Who's he?"

Rhea whispered, "Luther McIntire."

"I didn't think there was any corn to sell around here," I said.

"There isn't at regular prices. But McIntire's hoarded his back to sell for whiskey when it got short. That way he can get twenty-five or thirty dollars a bushel," Rhea explained.

"But people were starvin'."

"Ssh," Rhea said. "Let's find a way out of here home. We'll find you another bee gum."

Barely breathing we slipped away from the ridge and off Frolley's land toward the road. We finally felt safe enough to sit down. "You mean McIntire let his neighbors starve to make more money?" I asked.

"That's what it looks like," Rhea said. "But he'd not see it that way. He'd say it's his corn to do with as he pleases, and he's free to sell it for the best price. Other folks, he'd say, have the same opportunity, if they are smart enough."

"That isn't right, is it?" I asked.

"It isn't right for some to profit at other's

expense. But there's no one to stop it. The governments set prices, but a man can find his way around governments if he knows how. God, I guess, isn't so easy to fool," she said.

I heard two pops from down the road. "That's gunshots!" I said.

Rhea and I stood up and walked cautiously toward the sound. There in a timbered bend of the road was McIntire's empty wagon. McIntire crawled on the ground holding his stomach. A man came out of the brush. He walked up to McIntire as he crawled and stuck his pistol behind McIntire's ear and pulled the trigger. My eyes blinked at the concussion in the ravine. I felt Rhea's hand tighten on my shoulder. McIntire jumped like a killed calf and fell on his side. The killer rolled him over with his boot and pulled the money sack from his shirt. He straightened up and started away from us.

"Crysop!" Rhea called out hoarsely. The killer turned. It was Sweet William Crysop, and he was smiling at Rhea. "Are you so sure you can kill without being called to account?"

"No one has yet," he said.

Rhea had stepped away from me out into the road. I saw her raise the .36 Colt she carried since the Adler incident in the back of her skirt belt. Crysop tried to shoot, but he was too late. Three shots from her Colt hit him squarely in the chest. He spun away, falling face down in the road dust. Rhea walked to McIntire. He was dead. She went toward Crysop, and I started out. She turned.

"Stay there," she said to me.

Just then a bullet whistled past her head. She dropped to her knees and brought up the Colt. A second bullet smashed into the ground beside her. Rhea quickly put two rounds into the brush across the road. It was quiet then. She waited, holding the gun. Finally she stood up and walked across the road. I ran after her, catching up Crysop's gun as I passed his body. Rhea and I stood together looking into the ditch.

"You're a good shot, Missus Dameron. I shouldn't have missed you twice like that," Blackie Foard said. "I believe you have killed me. Crysop's not going to take you killin' his boy light." Foard slumped back against the ditch. His gun slipped out of his hand. Rhea picked it up by the barrel. When she stood up I saw tears running down her cheeks, and her jaw was set hard.

"I liked Foard. He had me fooled," she said

and reached into her skirt pocket. She brought out the pouch of minie balls. "Gilstrap was right, after all. Foard was the informer." She dropped one of the bullets beside Foard's head. We went back to Crysop and put another one there. There were three minie balls left in her hand.

Rhea took McIntire's money. I stepped in front of her. "That's stealing," I said.

"That's compensation," she said. "Owed a woman and six starving children who walked to Missouri because their neighbor wouldn't sell them a bushel of corn.

13

RHEA DAMERON was up early the day following our run-in with Blackie Foard and Sweet William Crysop. She had her horse hitched to the buggy and was leaving the yard when I jumped aboard.

"I'm going," I said. "Hillary said she'd finish my chores."

We drove out of our valley and through the mountains, making our way to the old Butterfield Road that ran from Van Buren to Fayetteville. Actually the old mail road ran from St. Louis to San Francisco, but those places seemed far away, like the moon, that day. We were out of time, out of the flow of larger things that morning. There were no great issues or ideas. There was only the question of Crysop and how he would take the death of his son.

Rhea stopped the buggy at Mrs. Norman's house. Mrs. Norman was a widow who supported herself and her children by sewing and keeping boarders. She was much respected among the women of our community.

"Wait here, please," Rhea said, and took a basket from the buggy and went inside. I fidgeted on the leather seat and put my bare feet on the front panel of the buggy. If we'd kept to the main street, I thought we could already have been to the store. We would know about the bodies, about Crysop. Rhea finally came out, with Jenny Norman following her.

"Thank you for the produce and eggs," Jenny said as Rhea climbed up. "I'll have that room fixed up before Sunday."

Rhea nodded, and we drove off. "What room?" I asked.

"Mrs. Norman has an extra room now. Claudia's been wanting to move into town. This will be a good time. You and Sarah will like playing with the Norman children. You need to be with people your own age," Rhea said.

"You're trying to get rid of us!" I said. "You're breaking your promise to Pa."

"It's not for good, son. It's just for a little while," Rhea said.

"I won't stay," I said. "I'll join the army or run off."

Rhea stopped the team. "Hush," she said.

"You know as well as I do what happened yesterday. Crysop's going to be riding hard, trying to find out who killed his son. It won't be safe at Vineyard. You don't want Sarah in danger do you? Of course not." She answered her own question.

"Sarah can come to town, but I'm staying," I said.

"John Luke, if you stay, I'll have you on my mind. Crysop could use that against us," Rhea said.

"If you know he's coming why don't we all stay in town together? He'd be scared to come after you here."

"We have animals and crops to take care of at Vineyard," she said.

"Walter England could take care of things."

"Not this time of year. He's got his own place to run. Besides Crysop could kill him just like Edd Huggins. I won't put England in that danger," Rhea said.

"How'd you know Crysop even wants you?" I asked.

"He doesn't—yet. That's why we can make our arrangements."

We stopped at the general store. There was a crowd around McIntire's wagon, but Rhea wouldn't let me look inside. McIntire, Crysop, and Foard were laid out, waiting for the old man Crysop to arrive. Rhea and I went into the store. Everybody was talking about the killings. Rhea passed the time, but didn't show much interest in the conversation. She was set on buying me a new pair of pants, Sunday pants, so I could be presentable living in town. She'd hold up a pair and consider them while the ladies told her about the killings and how no one was safe. She'd agree and pick another pair.

"Try these," she said at last, and sent me toward the storeroom.

I couldn't get my old pants off fast enough and into the new ones. The new material was stiff. It was hard to shove the buttons through the holes. "Damn," I said as the button popped back out the hole. I gave it another try as I started back to hear more of the adults' conversation. Rhea had moved to the mail window. She was mailing a small package. The name on it was Dela Andersen, Pineville, Missouri. Now that the Federals held Arkansas and Missouri, mail service was fairly reliable. The postmaster found Rhea's mail then, and handed it to her. There was a flat brown package and a letter.

She tucked them under her arm and turned to me.

"Stand over there, and let me look at you," she said. I did. "Turn around." I did. "What do you think?" she asked Mr. Elmore, the storekeeper-postmaster.

"He's of an age to grow fast," he said, scrathing his ear. "I reckon they're a little big at the moment, but on the long haul they'll be just fine. They'll set to him some after they're washed, too."

"Fine," Rhea said. "We'll take them and some undershorts and socks, too." I grimaced. Rhea wouldn't want me mentioning *her* underdrawers out loud in a crowded store. "Help me find a dress for Sarah," she said. We found one after looking through every single one twice, maybe three times. We also got the suitable underpinnings and stockings. Shoes were dear in those days so we did not buy them. In summer we went barefoot. Rhea hated that on account of the hook worms native to our Arkansas soil. She dosed us liberally and regularly for them. In fall and spring, Walter England made us each a pair. My Easter shoes were still good.

"We'll pay out now, Mr. Elmore," Rhea said. "Looks like business is good."

"No, Rhea," Elmore said. "Business isn't good. Folks are just standing and talking. So much talking keeps the buyers away from the counter."

"People are excited over the killings," Rhea said.

"It's Crysop they're thinking about. When news spread Sweet William was dead, everybody said, 'Thank God.' Next they wanted to see the body. Now they want to know what the old man is going to do. He'll play hell, beg pardon, that's what he'll do," Elmore said.

"He hasn't arrived yet?" Rhea asked casually.

"He'll be here anytime," Elmore said, folding my new pants. Rhea didn't say anything. She counted out the money for our clothes. Elmore wasn't finished. "Another thing," he said. "Blackie Foard being with Crysop, and both having minie balls by their heads, has settled who told where to find the conscripts. Looks like Gilstrap was right, after all, on that account."

"Yes. Yes, Gilstrap was right," Rhea said, and took her change.

215

"Thank you, ma'am," said Elmore, as we took our packages and went toward the door.

"Where'd the money come from for our clothes?" I asked.

"From Colonel Jamie Dameron," she said.

The next business down one door from the store was the mortuary and the McIntire wagon full of dead men. The next business the other way was the newest enterprise in town, the photographer, Paul Darwood. Darwood was an unnaturally skinny fellow without much hair. He always wore a striped shirt which was too big, with garters to keep the sleeves held up. At the moment, he was up on a crate pointing his camera down into the wagon.

"Take McIntire out of there. He wasn't no raider," someone in the crowd said. Some of the men took McIntire inside the funeral parlor. The photographer came down from the crate and off the porch to direct the arrangement of Sweet William and Foard for his camera.

"Who has the bullets?" he asked. Jesse Branch, the undertaker, handed them to him. He sat them carefully by each man's cheek. Finally, he climbed back to his perch and, after a few more adjustments, made his picture.

Darwood's picture became famous and was

printed in a number of books later. Everytime I see it, I'm caught by the barbarism of that time of quick death. I do not think I am ever sorry the two men are dead. They had earned their wages, but I think it strange now how callous we were to their death's privacy. We took all death seriously, grimly, intimately, but not privately. Somehow privacy was not much thought of in our small towns. We all knew each other too well, like a family without secrets among members.

There was a sense, too, that these men had forfeited something by their actions. Perhaps it was our sympathy, or respect. In our naivete we photographed death to hold a moment in time close. We did not, of course, anticipate our own mortality in the fact of the picture's immortality. All that remains for the casual viewer today is a grisly portrait of two lifeless men and the sleeves and arms and hat brims of those leaning against the wagon. There is no meaning for the viewer but what is written in the captions. "Sweet William Crysop and Blackie Foard, guerrillas, shot down June 14, 1863, by unknown assailants."

Sometimes the captions are cute or witty, "Swift Justice" or "Arkansas trial methods."

Sometimes Crysop and Foard are innocent victims of assassins. The casual viewer turns the page quickly to avoid the detail or lingers in morbid fascination. How many see the little minie balls and wonder why they are there? None remembers how Blackie Foard walked and talked that day Rhea and I bought the goats. None smells the odor of burning flesh when Sweet William ordered the Adler place burned with Mrs. Adler, Sally, and Toby locked inside. The viewer clicks his teeth and shakes his head and wonders how we could have killed these men and taken the picture. It is not Blackie Foard or Sweet William who are indicted, then, but our time. And we are envied for swift justice or shunned for our cruelty and unenlightened humanity. And the casual viewer does not know our conflict, our choice, our questions, or our reality as he looks at the flat grey picture in the lifeless books.

Eleazar Crysop descended on Prairie Grove as Rhea and I headed toward the buggy. He and his horsemen churned up the dust of the street as they rode at a gallop into the devastated town. Captain Dwight from Fayetteville was by Crysop's side. That fact made me shudder in the warm breeze. Rhea and I waited silent and alone as Crysop rode his horse into the crowd around the wagon. He looked at his son, studied the colorless sunken features.

"Turn him over," he said to the undertaker. "I want to see the holes in his back."

"He wasn't back shot," Jesse Branch said.

"He was shot from behind," the powerful man said. "No bullet was ever made that could kill a Crysop head-on. No man could face a Crysop down and live."

The undertaker laid his palm over young Crysop's chest. "There's three shots in the space of my hand," he said. "All dead through the heart. They killed him, all right."

"Those are exit wounds," Captain Dwight said, without looking at the body.

Crysop saw the minie balls then. "What the hell's that?" he asked, but he knew. "Who put those abominations by my innocent child?"

"We found them beside the men where they were killed," Branch said.

The captain looked at the bullets. "Like the one's found by the two partisans near Fayetteville?" he asked.

"I wouldn't know that," said Branch. "They were just there by the bodies. Seemed to be marking them. We figured these two were robbing Luther McIntire when somebody called them out."

Crysop did not listen to Branch's speculation. He rose in his stirrups and turned about the crowd. His voice thundered over our heads, and inside I began to shake. "Someone's marked himself," he said. 'I'll find ye out. And better for ye ye were never born than the day I find ye." His black suit seemed to wrap him in a sober power. 'I'll find ye out! Ye'll bleed for your treachery," he said. "This land will run blood till my boy's murderer is found. Do ye hear me? Bring me the murderer, and I'll spare the rest of ye." The crowd had drawn away from Crysop when he rode in, but by the time he finished his speech, it was tight against the buildings blown away by the concussion of his words, yet held by the perimeter of the street.

"Jesus Christ," a man whispered beside us.

"We've posted a thousand dollar reward for the killer," Dwight said. "Bring us a name and the money is yours."

I felt then that Rhea was already dead. I was powerless, grieving already for her. I looked up at her. She was standing straight with her head up. If she was afraid, I could not tell. She watched him closely, the black-clad, white-haired patriarch of Hell. Then she turned away. As we walked toward the buggy, I heard a man in the crowd say softly to his neighbor, "It's a fair trial the man whose name comes forth will get!" Then he spat in the dirt. Rhea and I climbed into the buggy. We drove out of Prairie Grove with Crysop's thunder ringing in our ears.

14

RHEA and I rode in silence back toward Lord's Vineyard. Finally, I said, "Rhea, I'm scared, scareder than I've ever been."

"Are you scared of Crysop or for me?" she asked.

"Scared of what Crysop will do to you."

"Well," she said. "Crysop's a dangerous enemy and not to be taken lightly. But he's not perfect. Evil's an imperfection, a flawed creation. He has a weakness somewhere. We'll just have to watch for it and hope it shows."

"Rhea, he's going to kill you," I said.

She drove on. "He's going to try," she said quietly.

I remembered how Rhea had stepped out on Sweet William. She'd been safe in the brush, but she stepped out and called to him. "What do you think about when you face somebody who can kill you?" I said.

"At first I'm scared. More scared than you are now. Then, I get mad at my fear. I think

222

about what happens if I don't do something, not just to me but to somebody else who's old or weak. And my hands become steady. I see nothing, hear nothing but the deathdealer. I become a single purpose, a killing purpose. Time seems endless. I see every action, every movement slowly and deliberately. I don't know anything else until the barking guns awaken me.

"Boy," she said, "why don't you unwrap the package?"

She wanted to take my mind off Crysop and killing. I fumbled with the string and brown paper. Inside the paper was a box. Inside the box was a framed picture of Jamie Dameron. He wore his uniform. The buttons and braid shone. He wore a heavy thick mustache, carefully clipped. He was not handsome, that was for lesser men; he was commanding, a presence even there in that little frame. He looked the camera straight in the eye with his own tired, but steady gaze. You trusted Jamie Dameron to know what was right.

"I wish he was here," I said.

"So do I," Rhea said.

Crysop was true to his word. That very night,

he paid a visit to Gilstrap, but Gilstrap was long gone knowing that Crysop would look him up first. Crysop hit the Grahams' next. Like Gilstrap, the brothers were gone ahead of him. After that, Crysop turned mean. He looked for anyone who might tell him who killed Sweet William and the other partisans. He renewed his terrorism against us. He burned out a couple of the Grahams' neighbors and killed their stock. But no one could tell him anything because no one knew who had done the killing. Rhea was caught then between the danger to her neighbors and her own danger. She sent a letter to Captain Dwight by Walter England, protesting the raids that Crysop had renewed and redoubled. Dwight's response said simply that in war drastic measures must be taken against civilian populations who resist the conquering army. Soldiers could not be killed without retribution on the general population until they gave up the killers.

Rhea made up her mind then, I think, to turn herself in. But she still had to make arrangements for the rest of us. Saturday morning, Rhea loaded Claudia and Joey and Sarah and me in the buggy. I drove the horse she'd saved from the battlefield. I felt pretty good about the driving, but not about leaving Vineyard. I didn't want to be safe in town. I wanted to be with Rhea and Hillary at the farm.

Crysop's men had moved into Prairie Grove. There were only seven of them counting the replacements, but they were a big presence. There was no one in town for a Saturday. It was quiet. Rhea unloaded us at Jenny Norman's and helped us get settled. I bunked with Bob Norman, and Sarah was in with his sister. Claudia had the front bedroom to herself with Joey. Mrs. Norman made us a good lunch with the food Rhea brought from the farm. Afterwards, Rhea and I walked out in the backyard. The air was still and fresh. An old walnut tree gave a lacy shade of dark green over the bright green and sunshine lawn. I felt like I was dying. There was a pain as tight and hard as a fist in the center of my chest, and my throat hurt, too.

"I don't want to stay here," I said.

"I know," said Rhea. "I don't want you to stay. I've gotten used to you and Sarah. You are my own. And that's why you must stay at least a little while until things are settled."

"Rhea, I could help at Vineyard. You'll need someone to watch for Crysop. I can do that. I can shoot now, too."

"No," she said. "You don't need to have killing on your mind. You're getting big, but that's a weight too heavy to carry. I know. Did you bring your books?" I nodded affirmation. "If you need any more, you can go over to Papa's house and get them. You know where they are in the infirmary."

"I hate Crysop," I said. "Hate him!"

Rhea turned me to her and sat down on a stump. "John Luke, it might be you've seen enough and lost enough to have that right. But I want you to think about something else. A human heart is like a house. If the rooms are filled with bitterness and hate, there isn't any room for love and happiness. I'd feel better if you'd start to clean out those rooms that are full of bad memories. You can't do it all at once, but little by little, you'll make room for better things. I'm going to try to do that. I've got some things to do soon." She looked off in the distance. "Whatever happens, I love you and Sarah. I want you to be happy. I don't want you to have any bitterness about what may happen. I'm going to do what must be done. Hillary knows what to do for you if the time comes."

I wanted to ask Rhea what it was that she

had to do, but I think I knew. Before I asked, Jenny Norman called out from the back door. "Rhea, come quick!"

Rhea dropped the twig she'd been breaking, and we both ran to the door. Inside stood one of Crysop's partisans. He seemed to fill the whole room although he was not a big man.

"Andrew Crysop's been shot down. He's at the store," he said. "Someone seen your buggy here and said you could help."

Rhea and I followed the partisan. I brought along the bag. The man wasn't much more than three or four inches taller than Rhea, but he was stout, broad across his chest and shoulders. Neither of them talked as they walked down to the store. The dry dust rose from the street, coating their boots and Rhea's long skirt. She was grim beside the partisan.

When we reached the steps at the store, Crysop was waiting. It was the first time I had seen him close up or studied him. Everything about him was black as I looked up, black boots tucked in black pants, black gun belt over black coat. Everything was black except his dirty white shirt and white beard and hair. His eyes fixed us in the street. I had never seen eyes like his and shall never forget them—black and small, totally penetrating, burning with fanatical zeal, bereft of compassion or understanding. His mouth set tight in the white beard as he looked us over.

"Are ye the healer?" Crysop asked Rhea. She nodded. "Have ye a doctor's papers, woman?"

"No," she said. "I am not a doctor. I can sometimes help, but I am not a diploma physician. There are two in Fayetteville. They will come here if sent for."

"My nephew'll die if I wait for a doctor," Crysop said. "Do what ye can."

He stepped aside then, and let us pass into the store. Crysop's nephew was stretched out on the counter where cloth was measured. Some of the new bright bolts were under his head. Another lay in the floor stretched out and used to mop up the bloody path from the door. Rhea looked at the man's face, pale against the dark beard. She raised his eye lid gently. She felt the artery in his neck.

"When did this happen?" she asked, rolling up her shirt cuffs.

"Hour or so ago," the partisan who came for us said.

Rhea lifted away the bloody shirt and looked for the wound. She concentrated on the work, oblivious to Crysop, the raiders, and the store-keeper around her. "John Luke, bring some water. We'll clean this up some and see where we are."

"Get the water, Frank," Crysop said to one of the men and pushed me back beside Rhea.

The bullet had ripped into Crysop's nephew's lower back, exploding the black powder left in his flask. He was in bad shape from the wound, loss of blood, and long ride to town. But the explosion had not done as much damage internally as it might have.

"Hold the chloroform, John Luke," Rhea said, handing me a wad of cotton and the chloroform. She turned young Crysop's head, put the cotton over his nose and mouth, and began to drop the liquid into the cotton. "All right, son," she said to me. "Keep giving a little at a time. Remember don't breathe it in, or we'll pick you up off the floor next."

"Let one of my men do that," Crysop said.

"The boy knows how," Rhea said, as she watched me.

Rhea scrubbed her arms and the wounded man's side. In a little while she lifted the man's arm. It fell back loosely. That was our test in those days. When the patient was limp, it was safe to go to work. Rhea stopped the bleeding, tying off the vessels, and retrieved the lead and fragments lodged in Andrew Crysop. The bullet was a round ball. It had nearly turned itself inside out on impact. She rubbed morphine into the wound and seared flesh. Finally she sewed him up. Rhea liked for any wound to breathe or reach the air when possible, so she did not bandage Crysop, but merely covered the area and wrapped him in clean blankets from the store's shelves. In a little while we sat down to wait while Andrew Crysop decided to live or die.

The old man Crysop watched intently throughout the operation, but he did not speak until we finished. "What figure ye his chances?" he asked.

"He's young," Rhea said. "His heart and lungs are strong. That favors him."

Crysop took a seat in a rocker his men brought in from the porch. He had another brought in for Rhea. They rocked steadily back and forth on the pine boards, making a soft music as the afternoon slipped into twilight. Crysop studied Rhea intently, but she did not waver beneath his gaze as she fanned slowly and steadily with a palm leaf fan. Occasionally she got up to look at Andrew Crysop, then returned to the chair. Once Crysop went outside for a few minutes. Mr. Elmore came over to Rhea quickly.

"Don't let that boy die, Mrs. Dameron," he said. "He's all Crysop's family that's left. If he dies, he'll burn the town."

"Did your wife sell the pillow cases she had ready to embroidery last week?" Rhea asked. Elmore shook his head. "Good. I like to keep my hands busy," Rhea said. "Would you get it for me, please. And a package of needles, too."

Elmore brought the cases, bright thread, scissors, and needles. Rhea cut and separated a length, threaded a needle and began to pierce the material. In no time a bright pink blossom of loops appeared on the cloth. Elmore returned to his stool behind the counter long before Crysop came back.

Crysop sat back in the rocker facing Rhea and watched her even more intently. He rocked steadily. Rhea rocked and sewed until it was too dark and she sat the work aside.

"Mr. Elmore," she said. "We need some light now." Elmore began to fuss with the lanterns. Still Crysop sat staring at Rhea.

231

"My men say they seen ye before out at a slaver's place," he said.

"I've seen your men before, too," Rhea said.

"What were ye doing in such company?" he asked.

"The Adlers owned no slaves. I was in their company for the same reason I'm in yours, they needed me."

"My boys say you ain't scared of hell fire," Crysop said. "You ain't scared of me?"

"Have I reason to fear you, Mr. Crysop?" Rhea asked calmly, and I thought of Sweet William lying in the wagon dead in front of the funeral parlor.

"There's those who fear me," the old man said.

"I'm afraid of many things, Mr. Crysop, but I fear most things I cannot see," Rhea said. "Things inside like doubt and fear and hate. Things inside the heart and mind are dark and treacherous and hidden. It's better to see your adversary."

"So it is, woman," Crysop said. "But what's on the inside will be on the out. Take slavery. There's a pernicious evil, a darkness inside men. But their dark ways mark them, and I

232

find them out. I know my enemy, and I kill him, anyway I can."

"You've never killed anyone innocent?" Rhea asked.

"Never a one," the old man said. "On my Bible, never a one."

"Truly," Rhea said. "Adler had no slave, but his daughter and son died at your men's hands. Maude Pepper had no slave, but you broke her hands."

"There's those tainted by the toleration of slavery," he said.

"Then being white in this country makes us all guilty."

"That's the size of it," Crysop said. "Ye permitted it and that's your guilt."

"There are men here who hated slavery as much as you," Rhea said.

"Talk's cheap. Deeds live," Crysop said.

"A blue uniform doesn't make you right anymore than living in this country makes these people wrong. You've just replaced one evil with another," Rhea said. "The injustice endures, only the masters are different."

"Get us some grub, storekeep," Crysop said and sunk deeper into the chair. "Ye are a hard talkin' woman."

233

Rhea and I ate from our tray the food Elmore brought. It was good food. Crysop ate silently in his chair, studying Rhea, from time to time when he looked up from his plate.

"Storekeep," Crysop said. "Light the fire and boil the coffee. It's a long night comin'." Mr. Elmore kept a pot of coffee going on the pot-bellied stove. It made the store hotter in the summer night, but the coffee tasted good and kept us awake while we waited.

I went outside a couple of times, sat on the steps, and listened to the night sounds off in the distance behind the houses. Three of Crysop's men took their ease on the long porch. I knew the one called Frank and another one from the Adler place.

"I don't know how he stands that fire," one of them said. "Hot summer night like this and the old man sits there by a stove in a coat with a blanket around his shoulders."

"His blood don't circulate," Frank said. "He's a old man, and time's heavy on him since Will's murder. Sometimes he gets chills like tonight. Sometimes it's fevers. In Kansas I seen him fight ten men when he could barely hold a gun for shakin' from the chills." The others didn't say much for a while.

234

"Sure wish I was at home," one of the raiders said. "Nights like this I can taste Kansas. I'd be settin' on my porch with my wife and youngins listening to the air laying still on the fields. I can smell my land almost if I close my eyes."

"I'm going to get me a little place when this here war is over," Frank said. "I got me a woman picked out over to Bentonville. I want some kids, too."

"My boy's about his age," the first man said, gesturing toward me. "Where's your pa, boy?" he asked.

"Dead," I said and went inside. Saying the word helped me remember these men were not like everyone else even though they talked easily on a cool porch on a summer night.

I had not thought of Crysop's raiders as family men. I did not want to. I did not want to like them or get trapped by their humanity. I wanted to remember they were merciless killers who followed the old man and did whatever he bid. I did not want to be confused by liking them or understanding them. But I had learned something that night Rhea already knew. People were people with a little good in the worst and a little bad in the best. There were both sides even in the worst. That's what made decisions tough and imperfect. I wondered how God could ever sort out a man and add him up for good. But I knew what we had to do if we got pushed into it. I had to hold to that through all the other feelings or get swept away. Like Pa said, a man had to stand for something. This was what he meant.

When I went back in again, Rhea had made me a pallet on the counter out of blankets. I didn't want to go to sleep just then, but I lay down to rest and think. The rolled blanket-pillow was scratchy on my face, but pretty soon I forgot about it and closed my eyes. When I opened them again, Rhea was tending young Crysop. She gave him bread soaked in wine whenever he came around. She bathed his face and hands in cool water to comfort him. Crysop still rocked and stared, covered to his ears in the blanket. The hours passed on into night and early morning. Crysop dozed in his chair. Sometimes he came and looked at the wounded man. Sometimes he talked to Rhea. I could hear their distant voices among the rocking sounds, trailing off mysteriously like a dream in my present reality of sleep. Again and again I fought back to consciousness when their voices awakened me.

"Andy's all I got left of my blood folks," said Crysop. "He ain't smart like my boy, Sweet William, but I didn't raise him up. My brother's boy he is, like his father. It's the way a pup or boy's raised up. My brother never knowed that. Let Andy grow up loose in his thinkin', soft and easy. My boy, my boy was worth ten of him for savvy and sand. William was like me. The taste of slavery was bitter in his mouth. I taught him that. He never had to ask what to do. He knowed. He knowed 'cause he'd watched me and listened to me—everything just like me. When he's just a little fellar I'd look down, and he'd be trying to match his baby steps to my tracks in the sand. My boy's dead," Crysop said quietly. "The good die young."

I looked at Rhea's eyes watching Crysop's face. They were soft and sad. She started to talk softly, painting a picture. "Did you ever think what it would be like if people could live our their normal lives without somebody deciding to kill them or use them for some private purpose. Think of it, Mr. Crysop. Babies would be born into secure and loving families that ate the fruit of their own labor. Barns would be full with fresh paint on the outside and a good roof atop. Cattle and horses would be fat as they grazed grass in long meadows. In the house the women would smile and plan their quilts and their gardens between their chores. In summer they'd take lunch to the men in the fields and put the children down to sleep in the cool shade of the wagon. In winter the men would sit by the fire planning their next year's crops, knowing there was food laid by for their families and stock. And when life's sadnesses came, the neighbors and friends would care and help, and the burden would be lighter for the sharing and the love. People would worship God because it was the natural thing in their hearts, not because somebody said they had to in a certain way or somebody else said they couldn't. In their old age, they could look back on what they'd done and forward on what their children and grandchildren would go on to do. There'd be love and warmth and a place to be in that winter season, not bitterness. That's the way it's supposed to be.

"But some people, people like you, Mr. Crysop, can't let it be because of some sickness inside that makes them judge and covet and try to bend life to their omnipotent will, their plans. You're the tyrants deciding for other

238

people, bypassing law and consensus, unwilling to abide by the decision of good and thoughtful men, unwilling to persuade and change men's minds, quick to kill and terrorize in your burning self-righteousness.

"There isn't an all right or an all wrong, Mr. Crysop. No man can claim that for himself or put it off on another. But there is something bigger. There's love and forgiveness and compassion and simple kindness. When a man goes against those, he's forfeit. One of these days people are going to realize that killing and dying are too small and private in the scheme of things, too ineffective. Someday we've got to make a front so big and so strong and so solid no killer can break it. Not even you, Mr. Crysop. Don't you know nobody can ever hurt his neighbor without robbing himself, that you're a poorer man for the hell you've caused? It just seems to me there are enough natural pains in life without people going out of their way to make more."

My eyes were wide open by the time Rhea finished. I figured Crysop would come out of his chair and shoot her dead on the spot. But he didn't. He just rocked, caught up, I guess, in Rhea's vision and sincerity, and the harsh reality of burned out farms and busted up families and women and kids starving to death because of it.

"Where's your man, woman?" he asked.

"In the East," she said.

"Butternut?" Crysop said.

"No. He's a colonel of Union cavalry," she said.

"Where'd you learn healin'?" he asked Rhea.

"From my father," she said. "He was the village doctor here."

"What become of him?"

"He was killed by a raider named Crysop," she said steadily, looking into Crysop's black shining eyes. "Expertly executed with five wounded men in a cave."

"Take care, woman," Crysop warned. "I'm beholdin' to ye thus far, but I'll not be chided by a female for doing my duty."

Before Rhea could answer, the man on the counter moaned. She bent over him. He was awake. "Uncle," he said. Crysop came to him. "Uncle, they ain't scared no more. They're fighting back."

Rhea touched the man's forehead. "Ssh," she said. "You can talk another time. You must try to get this down and gain strength." The raider drank the broth she offered.

"My back is on fire," he said.

"Somebody said once as long as it hurts, you can tell you are still alive. That doesn't help much, but it is true. This will help the pain," she said, easing a needle into his flesh. Rhea changed the wet clothes, dipped them in fresh water, rung them out with her hands, and reapplied them to his back. When she finished she turned to Crysop. "He's strong," she said. "He'll feel worse in a couple of days, but I believe he will recover if you see he rests. By morning you can move him gently to the hotel. You should send for a doctor. There's time now."

Rhea rolled down her sleeves and began to gather her things. Crysop said nothing, but rocked steadily in the shadow beside the door. As we walked toward the door, he put his foot out and blocked us.

"Who killed my boy?" he asked.

"I did," said Rhea.

Crysop looked at me. The lantern light reflected from his eyes. "Your boy?" he said softly, spreading his big hand across my chest like the undertaker had done on Sweet William. Rhea pulled me away. I felt her hand shaking

241

as she held me. I did not know if it was from fear or anger. "Frank," Crysop said. "See the woman gets safe home. I owe her a small favor." Frank walked with Rhea and me down the steps, but Crysop called us back. "Woman," he said. "Come morning, I'll come for ye and your boy. Everyday I don't find ye, one of the folks here are going to suffer. They'll help me find ye when they know you're the reason. And when I find ye, ye'll give me your boy for mine. Ye'll give him to me."

242

15

RHEA and I rode out of Prairie Grove in the darkness. We had one stop before we made for the high mountains —Lord's Vineyard. There we picked up supplies, our hidden guns and ammunition, and a saddle for the buggy mare I was riding. Hillary helped us with the calm and sure swiftness I had come to expect from the woman. She watched us leave from the porch.

Rhea looked around the place one last time from her saddle. No one, I thought, could have forced her out of Vineyard if it were not for me. She'd have fought Crysop if I were safe. She'd tried to arrange that, but Crysop had made her change her plans. We were fugitives now, driven out and hunted by an old man who'd found her weakness.

In less than an hour, we were over the ridge south then east into the highest hills and deepest valleys. Sunrise found us climbing among the verdant trees with the twisting valleys below in panorama. We kept in the trees

243

as much as possible avoiding the open valleys that might reveal us to our pursuers. Twice we stopped, resting the horses, watching the back-trail for Crysop's men, but we saw no signs of them. They knew the hills, as well as Rhea, and did not give themselves away to us. Rhea did not talk at all, she just rode, leading me to some destination only she knew.

We crossed every stream and rode down it sometimes doubling back to cover our trail. By nightfall we had ridden ourselves and the horses out. We made a cold camp in a ravine hidden by trees. I fell asleep almost at once clutching Pa's shotgun. When I awoke in the night, Rhea was gone. Her horse was grazing with mine. The blankets stuffed with limbs gave the appearance of her presence. I supposed she was sitting in the brush waiting for our pursuers, but when I called out she did not answer. I went back to sleep, then, too tired to worry or wonder. By sun-up, she still had not returned. I got up and saddled the horses. Still Rhea did not return. I ate my cold breakfast and waited. As the sun got higher, I toyed with the idea of going to find her, but let it pass. By noon, I took Pa's gun and headed back the way we had come, leading the horses. I walked for about an hour avoiding the open places again.

I did not know where I was going exactly, just back the way we'd come. Rhea had to have gone back to try and find the men following us. I guessed they must have caught her, or she'd have come back. If she was dead, they wouldn't care much about me. I had to think what to do. I was Sarah's only living relative, and she'd need me. Hillary would most likely stay with us. In another two or three years I'd be big enough to handle most farm work. Till then, we'd just get by, maybe rent out or go shares with somebody on our farm. It was free and clear. Like Rhea told Dela Andersen, we could hope on the land. Chances were Jamie Dameron would stand by us on account of Rhea's promise to Pa, but I didn't want to ask for help. We could manage. I'd learned a lot from Rhea.

I kept walking and thinking. About mid-afternoon, I found Rhea's straw hat in the path. I stopped, listening, watching for any movement. I went on after awhile, still alert but moving. I came around a bend that snaked back sharp to the left and there stood Frank and the other two partisans I knew from the porch at the general store. They saw me, too.

245

"Ain't that the kid?" Frank said.

"Yeah," said one of the others. They started to run toward me. I saw their guns come out of their holsters.

They were coming toward me yelling, spread out in a line from where they started. I saw it all plainly, clearly, almost in slow motion, like Rhea said it happened. I knew I had to get out of there, but fast as I tried to run I just stayed rooted to the rocky ground.

Suddenly, Rhea Dameron was in front of me, and the Sharp's rifle barked in her arms. She did not sight. She just pointed it and pulled the trigger. Frank went down on his knees, then, toppled forward. The fellow behind him fell, too. But the last man scrambled into the brush and up the hill. Rhea pushed me behind a rock and ran up the slope. I lay against the rocks listening to them running in the underbrush. I held the shotgun to my chest. I would not let Rhea down if my chance came, not this time.

I noticed the hill was quiet; nobody moved. Suddenly something moved to my left. I turned and fired. The next I knew Crysop's man was on me, and my shotgun lay in the rocky path. He had me by the neck and dragged me away from my hiding place toward the horses. I kicked and jumped, but his thick forearm was locked under my chin. I could see his horse pistol out of the corner of my eye pointing at my head. The hammer was back and his finger was on the trigger.

"The kid's dead," he said, "if you don't come out. Crysop wants him, but I'll kill him now."

The mountain seemed eternally quiet. Nothing moved, not a bird or rabbit or leaf. The raider jerked me again. I felt the cold muzzle of the .44 against my temple. He breathed hard from his run and the effort to hold me. For some reason, to emphasize his intent maybe, he turned the gun away from me and fired. The shot beside my ear deafened me and the powder burned my cheek.

I didn't hear Rhea's shot. I only felt the raider's weight as he pulled me to the ground. His arm pinned me to him, but I struggled out. There was one neat hole, center of his forehead, and he was dead. Rhea stood beside a forked tree, the Sharp's rifle smoked in her hands. My legs were shaking, so I sat down on a rock. I looked at my hands and pressed them against my knees to stop them from trembling. When

I looked up Rhea was there. She looked at me closely.

"Are you hurt?" she asked.

"I don't believe so," I said. "But I'm shaking pretty hard."

She smiled, then, and sat down beside me. "Me, too," she said. I could see her better, and her hands could barely set the Sharp's down. "Why'd you come down here?"

"I figured you were dead, and I ought to go back to Sarah," I said. "Where have you been?"

"I backtracked last night trying to find these fellows, but they stopped off at a farm house down the mountain for the night. I came back up here and waited. I saw you coming one way and them the other. The best I could do was throw the hat on the trail and try to get between you and them," she said.

The horses came up toward us. "Where to now?" I asked.

"I thought about that all night, John Luke. We're going back. We're not going to run and wonder who's behind us all the time. Crysop wants us running scared. That's his game. We are not going to play. This game is going to be as expensive for him as it is for us from now on. Everything he's won has been by fear. We've given him his best weapon, and he's used it."

"But Rhea, people are scared 'cause he kills and burns."

"That's true," she said. "But he kills and burns without resistance. The soldiers won't stop him. Women and children can't fight him. The men here are old or sick or unarmed. He's got a license. John Luke, we're scared because we are weak, not because Crysop is strong. But boy, somebody shot Andrew Crysop and nearly killed him. Somebody besides us is fighting Crysop now. With the guns we've taken, a lot of homesteads could defend themselves. If the will is there, boy, and I believe it is, if we can bring it out, Crysop's day will soon be over."

Rhea and I gathered the raider's weapons. They were always armed to the teeth with good pistols and rifles and plenty of ammunition. We unsaddled their horses and let them go. Finally Rhea dropped two more of the minie balls—one by Frank, one by the raider who had grabbed me. There was only one left now. Crysop's name was on it.

We rode away leaving the three bodies on the trail. Cutting across country, we intersected the

Butterfield Road outside Van Buren. It was dark when we rode down the hill into town. The courthouse and federal office lay at the bottom of the road by the river, but we stopped at the printer's. Rhea went upstairs to the living quarters of the owner, Franklin K. Beggs. Beggs had died in the war, but his widow still ran the paper and job printing. When Rhea reappeared Mrs. Beggs was with her, fully dressed and seemingly ready for the business that lay ahead. At the office we woke up the old press man who came to the door still rubbing his eyes.

"Lowell," Mrs. Beggs said, "fetch the boy. We have type to set and a special order to print. This is to be kept quiet for now." The old man grumbled about harebrained, pants-wearing women, but went after the printer's devil. Meanwhile Rhea took a seat at a desk in the office and busily dipped her pen in the ink as she wrote out the copy for the broadside and special edition of the Southwest Frontier.

She wrote for a long time. Mrs. Beggs took the first pages and gave them to the boy to set. Lowell prepared the press and fussed around a great deal about never getting any sleep. Mrs. Beggs ignored Lowell and made us a pot of coffee and sandwiches. She took other pages from Rhea and gave them to the boy. Sometimes she herself wrote and helped set pages.

I fell asleep from pure exhaustion sometime after midnight. When I awoke the old press was sliding smoothly back and forth in a contented rhythm. Rhea and Mrs. Beggs were bundling the broadsides with twine and stacking them. I picked up one of the loose sheets smudging the still wet ink with my thumb. It was tomorrow's edition of the Frontier. The front page carried the masthead and a banner headline: "Crysop Killer Confesses." Below was Rhea's confession.

"I, Rhea Isaacs Dameron, wife of Col. Jamie Dameron, U.S.C., shot and killed Sweet William Crysop and Blackie Foard on June 14, 1863.

My Ward, John Luke Pierce, and I had been coursing bees near the road when we heard two shots. When we arrived at the spot of the incident, Luther McIntire was crawling in the road on his hands and knees. A man who we did not then know stepped from hiding near us and went to McIntire. He put his pistol behind McIntire's ear and fired. McIntire fell dead. The killer bent over him and removed a money bag from McIntire's belt. I stepped from my own place and called out to the man I, then, knew to be Sweet William Crysop. He raised his pistol, but I shot him. He and McIntire were dead when I reached them. At that time my ward came out, and I turned to warn him back. Two shots narrowly missed me. I emptied my gun into the underbrush from which the shots came. After a time when no more shots occurred, we went to investigate. We found Blackie Foard dying. Before we left, I placed a minie ball by Foard and Crysop to show their complicity in the murders of the conscripts at Eden's Bluff. Crysop I had seen at the cave. Foard was indicted by the companionship with Crysop, his actions toward me, and his knowledge of the hiding place of the conscripts.

On December 11, 1862, about dawn, I saw six men emerge from the cave. I saw them clearly because of the lanterns they carried out of the cave with them. Two of these men I killed near Fayetteville after they attacked a refugee girl. Causing her to lose her unborn

252

child. I left minie balls by their bodies. Another of the killers came to my husband's farm at Lord's Vineyard. He was killed in a fall from his horse. Yesterday two more of the killers present at Eden's Bluff and a third I did not know died by my hand while they sought to track down and kill my ward and me. They, too, were marked by the minie balls. Only one remains. I give it the name of Eleazar Crysop, who executed five wounded men and my father Dr. Isaacs. I know his role from my own view of him replacing his gun in its holster outside the cave and from the dying testimony of Luke Pierce who was present inside the cave and saw the killings. The men killed at Eden's Bluff were loyal Union men who had refused to fire on the soldiers they were conscripted against. There was no military reason for their deaths at the hands of a Union partisan except the selfish gain to be had from their meager possessions and the blood lust of the man called Crysop.

Twice I have spoken with the Federal Captain in Fayetteville concerning this man and his murderers. I have offered to stand as a witness against him to no avail. But with this confession of my own guilt in several kill-

ings I witness to the character and guilt of Eleazar Crysop. I can be found at Lord's Vineyard by lawful authorities."

It was signed Rhea Isaacs Dameron and was followed by a list of the murders and burnings at which Crysop and his men were present, including the deaths of the conscripts, the unborn child, Toby and Sally Adler, and Luther McIntire. There were others, too, that Rhea knew through the people, but that I had not known.

By the time I finished reading the long confession, Rhea had carried some of the broadsides to the horses. The rest Mrs. Beggs would distribute. In the next hours, the flyers would be tacked up and passed out in Van Buren and Fayetteville, and in all the towns between by a network of citizens. Rhea's confession was Crysop's indictment. She had found his weakness—truth—even if it meant her own death.

"You should get some rest before you start back," said Mrs. Beggs as Rhea and I climbed aboard our horses.

"I'm anxious to get back," said Rhea. "I want to check the farm and my sister-in-law in Prairie Grove."

254

"Why Claudia came through here two days ago with some soldiers," Mrs. Beggs said and caught her mistake.

"Had they arrested her?" Rhea asked.

"It didn't look that way," she said hesitantly. "It looked like an outing."

"Was the baby with her?" Rhea asked.

"No. No children. Rhea, you must let that woman go her own way," said Mrs. Beggs.

"Where did she go?"

Mrs. Beggs plainly did not want to say. "Let it lay, child," she said.

"Where?" said Rhea.

"Miss Laura's on the Row," said Mrs. Beggs and went back inside.

Rhea turned her horse toward the river instead of home. We crossed the Arkansas in the dark by ferry. Before dawn we were in that seamy part of Ft. Smith that parallels the river. First the hangout of sailors on the river and the unsavory crowd their vices drew, it found new life with the soldiers and still later with the railroad men. Miss Laura's was still well-lighted. We saw two men leaving, swinging along happily toward the saloons as we rode up. A horse was tied at the rail out front. Rhea dismounted slowly and walked up the steps into the lantern light. She hit the door with her palm and a black haired woman clad in a corset, pantalets, and white painted face opened the door. "What the hell!" she said as Rhea pushed past her.

"Where's Claudia Isaacs?" Rhea said backing the woman against the door. "If you don't tell me I'll open every door in this damn place."

"Upstairs. Room seven," the woman said.

"Don't you move a whisker," Rhea said to her. "I've not got an ounce of patience left. I'd just as soon kill you as look at you." The woman froze. It must have been the deadly way Rhea said the words or the authority of right for she had no gun out to back her threat.

Rhea climbed the broad oak stairs slowly and made the turn with me behind her. I hung back a bit taking in the tassels and colors of Miss Laura's and staying far enough away so Rhea wouldn't send me out. I'd been waiting for Claudia's undoing, and didn't want to miss it. Rhea found room seven and opened the door without knocking. From behind her I saw a man and Claudia and heard Claudia gasp, "Rhea!"

"What's going on here?" he said.

256

"Get out," Rhea said not looking at his fat body.

He passed me in the hall carrying his clothes, wearing his hat. Rhea stepped into the room and closed the door. I couldn't see, then, but I heard her say in a low quiet voice. "Is this your choice, Claudia?"

"No. No." Claudia cried. "I was sold to that awful woman downstairs by a drunken soldier I thought planned to marry me."

"Get your clothes on," Rhea said. I heard the bed heave and Claudia scrambling around the room. "You left Joey to come up here with a soldier who said he wanted to marry you?"

"Yes. He was so attentive and gentlemanly," Claudia said. I guess she was fixing her face by the mirror because the next I heard was a crash of breaking glass and plaster.

"By God," Rhea said, "get away from there. Now listen to me very carefully, Claudia. We are going home, out of this whorehouse where you've come to roost. And you are going to be a perfect mother. You are going to be up early and late working to care for your little boy's every need. You are not going to smile or bat your eye at any man until you've grieved a long solid time for my brother. You aren't going to blow your nose without my permission till I decide to let you go for this. But when and if you do go, you will leave your son and my brother with a good name."

Claudia flew out the door nearly on top of me. And Rhea pushed her when she looked back. As we went out the door, Rhea spoke to the woman still frozen by the door.

"What did you pay for her?"

"Five hundred," she said.

"That's too much," Rhea said. "Consider it a loss on poor judgement. She's earned enough in two days to pay for this horse so we'll take it."

"But, Rhea, I can't ride astride. It's not lady-like," Claudia said.

Rhea looked at Claudia like she was a bug. "You get your dainty butt on that horse," she said. Claudia climbed right up. As we rode away, Rhea talked to herself. "I can't ride astride," she said mimicking Claudia and shaking her head. "Two days in a Fort Smith whorehouse, and she's too much a lady to ride astride!"

16

FROM Fort Smith we went home. We stopped off once somewhere in the hills at a cabin. I did not know the old woman who came to the door, but she knew Rhea. She also knew what to do with the raiders' guns we had taken and with the bundle of flyers we left.

We did not reach Vineyard until nightfall. There was a light burning in the kitchen. When we entered Hillary was cooking. There were plates for each of us sitting on the table and one of the confession flyers. The news had beaten us home.

"It's about time you got here!" Hillary said. "You must have come all the backways by snail."

I laughed out loud to hear her voice and to be home at Vineyard. We had come through the back country but we did not ride snails, we carried Claudia.

Claudia did not eat with us. She was too tired from the ride and her experiences of the last few days. Neither Rhea nor I lingered over the meal. I looked at Rhea across the table. She was almost asleep while she ate. Several times I had noticed her dozing on the horse as she rode in the afternoon. I had slept twice since she had, and I could barely keep awake. Rhea Dameron had come to the end. She had come home to rest. Hillary saw it, too. She helped Rhea up from the chair, and we guided her upstairs to bed.

When the bright sun awakened me the next morning, I felt fresh and renewed. I dressed quickly and went toward the stairs. Rhea's door was still closed as I passed. In the kitchen, Hillary sat at the table drinking what we called coffee and reading the flyer.

I pulled out the chair making a good racket. "Ssh, boy," she said. "She ain't awake and I don't want her waked up either. Sit down and I'll get your breakfast."

"Wait, Hill," I said. "I ain't too hungry, and I want to talk." She sat back and looked at me. "Where'd that flyer come from?"

"Walter England brought it over yesterday afternoon. Picked it up in Fayetteville," she said.

"You reckon everybody's seen it?" I asked.

"I imagine a lot of folks have seen it, and a

260

lot more have heard about it," Hillary answered.

"What do you think Crysop and Captain Dwight will do about it?"

"Mr. England said the captain was trying to figure out what to do. England said messages were burning up the telegraph wires. Somebody in Ft. Smith wired St. Louis and from there Rhea's story went to Washington. He said he thought Dwight would be relieved of his command and replaced and a warrant issued out for Crysop and his men before sunset. Things are humming around these tired old hills," Hillary said.

As we talked I heard a rider in the yard. We went to see. Through the curtains we saw it was Mr. Elmore from the store in town. We went outside to the porch. He didn't get off the horse. "Crysop's gone," he said. "He's gone back to Kansas with a troop of United States Cavalry on his heels. Praise God and that woman for getting rid of him. I got to get out to my brother's place with the news, but I thought you ought to know." He turned his horse sharply to the left of the porch, and handed Hillary a brown sack. "That's coffee,

261

real coffee, and some sugar. You all enjoy that," he said and rode off.

I did a cartwheel off the porch and jumped around in pure joy chasing old chickens and throwing rocks into the air with all my energy. Hillary did a little dance, too. But when I looked up at the house, I saw Rhea in the open upstairs window. She was not smiling.

When she came down to breakfast, Rhea was fresh and cheerful. We ate breakfast and lingered around the table drinking Mr. Elmore's coffee.

"Crysop's gone, really gone!" I said again and again, savoring the words and their meaning. Rhea smiled, but I felt there was something held back from the pure joy and happiness I felt. "What's wrong, Rhea? Are you worried about going to trial?" I asked.

"No," she said. "I just don't quite believe Crysop would leave. He's not a man to give up. He's his own justice, and I don't figure he's been paid. I think he'll be back for Sweet William's revenge."

"Aw, Rhea," I said. "He's scared now. Everybody's against him, not just the people, but the soldiers."

262

She smiled at me, but I had not changed her mind.

At Vineyard we had work to do. A farm cannot be ignored in the summer. Weeds and crops grow too fast. After breakfast Rhea set out to check things. She walked in the orchard. She saw to all the animals, curried, and fed our horses. She took her hoe and worked in the garden. Walter England came over after supper.

He'd washed his face and hands and combed his hair, but he still wore his work clothes. He and Rhea set a time to cut hay, and he went home. The days fell into a natural progression after that as we tended the needs of the land. A summons came for Rhea to appear in the August session of court, but she was not arrested. I began to forget about Crysop. He lost reality for me in the bright summer days, like a nightmare on a sunny morning. I worked on the farm, swam in the creek, and visited George England.

Even during war, people are still people, and when they can, they'd rather laugh than cry. George England and I even managed to become good friends. Rhea let me visit whenever she thought I had a legitimate invitation to stay overnight. And George was at our house often. We spent our leisure time fishing, idling away long summer afternoons watching our cane poles. By late afternoon, we'd gather our catch and head home. Sometimes we'd split up, each toward his own place, cutting across the wide green valley. Sometimes we'd both go to my house or George's.

George's father Walter was a Quaker, a quiet man who worked hard and skillfully. He helped us at Lord's Vineyard because he was a good neighbor. But Walter England had a streak—a streak of pure devilment—that revealed itself one summer twilight when I stayed to supper. We ate our meal with the pure delight and contentment of boys, hungry from fresh air, sunshine, and satisfying play. Mrs. England and Mrs. Pepper cleared away our empty plates, and we men adjourned to the porch. George and I sat on the steps and Mr. England eased his short spare frame into a rocker and began to rock comfortably as the twilight passed into darkness.

"Reminds me," he said slowly, "of the time when I first came out here, before I brought your mother here. I was wild in those days.

264

Bears and panthers were everywhere, and Indians," he added casually. "There weren't any good roads like there are now, no near neighbors, no wagons. A man had just his two feet, a horse if he was lucky, and a gun to get him game and keep him safe from the wild things.

"A trapper fellow moved in just in that hollow down there along the creek between this place and Dameron's." Walter England pointed across the land toward the spot. George and I strained to see the place in the faint remaining light. "He was kind of a smarty fellow. Came here to make his fortune and go back East to marry an important lady. At first everybody thought a lot of him, for he was a handsome and jovial man. But as they came to see his character, they began to cool in their opinion. And finally folks didn't like much at all for the way he took every good thing for himself.

"In a while they began to shun him because he'd borrow a pipeful of tobacco and keep the whole pouch—just tuck your pouch in his belt and walk off with it. They saw how he'd butcher a deer, take the best parts, and leave the rest to rot and draw wolves and panthers. The next day he'd kill another the same way.

265

Sometimes he shot at game birds and killed them just for sport.

"Well, when folks shunned him, he just got mad at them and stayed out by himself. He started hanging about the Indian people, trading with them. From the Indians he heard about a beautiful woman—a medicine woman who could make spells and ride the wind. Her place was up over the ridge somewhere in a secret cave where she lived with a mixed pack of wolves and panthers." I knew the exact spot. "Anyhow the Indians warned him off the woman. But the more he thought how beautiful she was and how she had magic powers to make a spell to make a man rich, the more he had to have that woman. So he set out. And he found her, all shining and bright, weaving out in front of the cave with the wolves and panthers lying about her feet. So he presented himself real nice. And he started to come back everyday, just polite and passing the time. And she came to like him for she'd never seen his bad side. And she told him her secret, that her powers were contained in the hairs of her head. Each time she made a spell, she'd pull out a hair, and throw it in the fire, and whatever she wanted, it'd come to pass.

"Well, the trapper got to thinking about that magic hair. He thought about that hair day and night and what he could do if he had that magic hair. So one day he went to her and said he'd like to buy a lock of hair. But she said she couldn't sell her hair because it belonged to the gods and she could only give it away to do good. So he went away and thought some more, and he decided to kill her and scalp her. He slipped into her camp, past the wolves and panthers because they'd gotten used to him. He went inside the cave and stabbed her through the heart and started to take her scalp, but his knife wouldn't cut it. He tried again and again, but he couldn't. He could pull out a single hair, but not cut the scalp. Then he figured it out. You had to take the magic hair one strand at a time. He cut off the woman's head and put it in a sack, walked past the guard critters who'd let the woman down, and went home. He felt pretty proud. While he was walking, he pulled out a long hair and set it afire from his pipe. He said he wanted a new rifle, and there it was in his hand." George and I were impressed with the wonderfulness of wishing for a rifle and getting it.

"The trapper," Walter England continued,

"could see what he had then—a key to a rich future where he could get anything he wanted whenever he wanted without working for it. When he got home, he hung the sack with the severed head in it by the door and went to bed. He started to plot and plan what he'd do with all that hair. There were things to get and people to get rid of, people who'd not treated him just right. He decided to remember everyone of them, every little thing anybody had ever done against him. With the hair he would repay each one in kind and more, insult for insult, eye for eye. He thought and thought until he finally fell asleep with the daylight. He slept all day, tired out from his night's labor and all his heavy thinking. He woke up at dusk about like it was when we came out here. He went to the bloody sack, reached in and pulled out a single hair. He threw it in the fire and wished himself a fine dinner with fiddle music. And so it was. He ate and drank long into the night, listening to his fiddle play by itself on his bunk, content with what he'd done. After a while he saw he was out of tobacco and wished he had some. But it didn't come because he needed another hair from the medicine woman's head for another wish. So he went back to the

268

bloody sack and got it. As he did he began to fret. He came to resent the need to go back each time he wanted to make a new wish. That thought began to play on his mind—everytime he wanted anything, he'd have to get a new strand of hair. That might not always be convenient. His magic began to look like work. While he thought how to get around the heavy labor, he heard a knock at his door." Walter England knocked on the chair arm, and George and I jumped at the sound.

"'Who's there?' the trapper asked. But there was no answer. 'Who's there?' Still no answer, just another knock. 'Tell me who's there or I won't open my door.'

"The head in the sack by the door began to wiggle. The trapper backed away. The head said in the woman's voice, 'My body has come for my head. Give back my head.'" Mr. England imitated the high spooky medicine woman's voice, drawing out the last word.

"'No!' the trapper said. 'Tis mine now.' He grabbed the sack and ran out the back. The headless body and the wolves and panthers came running behind him.

"As he ran, the head in the sack said, 'Give back my head.'

"He ran and they ran through the night over the hills. Behind him he heard the panthers' screams." Mr. England screamed like a panther. "When he looked back he could see their eyes shining red and their long white fangs dripping saliva. He remembered how a panther can slip up behind and cut the tendons in your neck with one bite.

"'Give back my head. Give back my head of magic hair,' the voice said from the bag." Again Mr. England made the shaky spook voice. I swallowed hard.

"Finally the trapper could stand no more. He could barely breathe. His legs were heavy like lead. And still they came. And still the head said, 'Give back my head of magic hair.'

"He flung the sack high up into the air out over the ridges and fell to his knees. The woman's headless body streaked past. But the wolves and panthers stopped and circled him, snorting and screaming, smelling his blood as they waited." Snorts and screams came from Walter England's mouth. "He started to run through a hole he saw, but a giant bear rose up out of the darkness."

I stood up. "I got to go now, Mr. England," I said, trying to sound normal. "Rhea won't

270

know where I am so late. Thanks for the good meal, Mrs. England." She and Mrs. Pepper had settled on the porch sometime during the tale. Mrs. Pepper ducked her head and dabbed at her eyes with her apron. I heard Mrs. England say, "Shame on thee, Walter," as I went down the steps.

There is no darkness like the darkness of a mountain valley where there is no moon. As I walked home through the dark across the field, I told myself it was a story Walter England had told, a made-up story with no truth. I was doing fine until I crossed the little bridge where Mr. England had pointed. Just as I put my foot on the wooden planks and heard the first hollow sounds of my feet above the creek, England's mule snorted in the brush. I could feel the warm panthers' breathe on my neck. And I ran. I ran hard and fast across the black night, forsaking mere breathe for life. Somewhere I realized it was a mule's snort, but I was unable to stop. I ran off the ridge above our place, sliding, striving for the porch light and safety. And just as I began to believe I'd make it, a massive shape stood up in my path. A rough hand grabbed me, "Slow down, boy. You've no

271

reason to be afeared." I looked straight into Ned Frolley's whiskers, and then, I ran.

I hit the back porch and collapsed, gulping air, holding on to the post. Rhea came outside. "Ned Frolley's on the ridge," I said at last.

"Must be coon hunting," Rhea said. "Come inside, John Luke." I went, but looked back under Rhea's arm. I did not hear any hounds with Ned Frolley.

I thought about Walter England's story and Ned Frolley, a lot during the next few days. I told Rhea the ghost story, and she smiled. I pointed out that Ned Frolley had no dogs. Rhea thought about that. Finally she said Maude Pepper's husband's sister, Earlene, was Frolley's mother, which made Mrs. Pepper his aunt by marriage, and he was probably on his way to the England place for a visit. That seemed reasonable, if complicated, and I thought no more about it. But to this day whenever I walk the hills and valleys, I'm alert for the bloody sack containing the medicine woman's head of magic hair that Walter England threw high into the air of my child's

272

mind. I'd hate to stumble over it even now.

Soon, a much more real, tangible terror confronted us. When Crysop rode over the north ridge into the yard at Vineyard, I ran for the house, but a raider cut me off and would not let me pass. They blocked Hillary, too. She was making soap on an open fire in the yard. Claudia and Sarah were in the house. I yelled for Rhea to run, but the raider knocked me down. He caught me by the back of my pants and hauled me across his saddle. I saw Rhea come to the porch and stand at the rail. She had a shotgun leveled at Crysop's broad chest. The raider carried me kicking to Crysop. He pulled out his pistol and cocked it against my head.

"Day to ye," the old man said. Rhea did not answer. "I'm speakin' to ye, woman. I expect an answer."

"Hello, Crysop," Rhea said.

"Do ye give me the boy?" he said.

"No," Rhea said.

"I promised ye'd give him to me, woman, when we next met. I expect ye'll do it before the day's over. Put down that gun, or I'll kill him." Rhea set the gun against the porch. "Come away from it," he said. "Down the steps

273

here." Rhea walked down the stairs into the yard. "Build up the fire," Crysop said to his men. Two of them slid down and tied their horses. They kicked aside the soap kettle and put more wood on the fire. "Tie up that nigger," he said, and another man bound Hillary.

Rhea did not take her eyes off Crysop. She watched him evenly without fear. I knew she was waiting for any opening and so did he. "Ye are quite the killer, ain't ye, woman. A little thing like you, fast and deadly like a mink. But I know ye. Ye won't make a fool of me. Boys tell me ye walked through fire at the Adler place," he said, holding me and the gun to my head. The pommel of his saddle stuck into the softness of my stomach, hurting me when I moved. "Bring the woman and me a chair," Crysop said. One of the men climbed to the porch and got the chairs. He sat Crysop's in the shade a few feet from the fire. Rhea's was in the sun next to the fire. "Get a bucket."

A bucket was taken from the kitchen and brought to him. "Fill it with live coals," Crysop said, and kicked loose his stirrups. He pulled me from the horse, holding the big gun to me and dragged me to his chair. He sat down

274

knocking me to my knees beside him. The gun never left my head. His holding hand moved from my neck to my hair. He jerked my head back.

"He's a good boy, woman. Sweet William was a good boy, I raised him good. But ye killed him. Now I miss my boy. I want a boy to raise up to take his place. Give me your boy for mine, and I'll get back on that horse and ride away back to Kansas. No harm will come to you or the boy. I'll raise him like my own; give him my wealth when I die. What say ye?" Crysop asked.

"No," Rhea said.

"I know he ain't your real blood boy. You can give him up easy," Crysop said.

"He is my son," Rhea said. "I will not give him up."

"Ye have sealed your fate," he said. "Bring the bucket." A man carried the bucket of burning coals to Rhea. Two men held her in the chair as they pulled off her moccasin and thrust her foot into the coals.

"Rhea!" I screamed. "Say yes!" She said nothing. Pain covered her face as the man held her foot and leg in the coals. "Let her go," I

275

said to Crysop. "Let her go. I'm my own boss. I'll go with you. Right now. I'll go."

"She took my boy. She must give me back her boy," Crysop said.

"I ain't her boy. I just live here," I said.

Rhea's face was wet with perspiration as the raider released her foot. She sighed heavily. "Fine boy," Crysop said. "He'll go far. Give him to me."

"No," Rhea said.

"She's rested long enough," the old man said, and his man stuck her foot back in the coals. Rhea's hands tightened on the chair. She pulled hard on them trying not to cry out. At last, she yelled. They released her. "Give him to me?"

"No," she whispered.

Again they pressed her foot into the coals. Rhea resisted until she passed into unconsciousness. "Get some water," Crysop said. One of the raiders brought water and threw it on Rhea. She awoke again. Crysop said to her again, "Give him to me."

"No," was again her answer.

Crysop studied Rhea. "Stand up," he said. Two men pulled her from the chair and held her before their leader. "Hold out your hands."

The men pushed her arms forward. "Palms up," Crysop said.

They turned her hands and pried open the fists. "She needs time to think," Crysop said. "Bring two burning sticks. Think about losing two healin' hands or one boy."

One of the men got the sticks from the fire. He trust them into Rhea's hands. The two released her. She strove to keep her balance on the burned foot. She started to fall, and I jerked away from Crysop. Rhea caught herself and brought the burning brands into his face. She held them to him as the chair fell backwards. Crysop's pistol fired into the air. He dropped it, and I grabbed it. He clawed at his face, at Rhea's hands, yelling for his men.

Suddenly shots rang out from the hill, hitting the dust by the three raiders' feet. They ran for their horses and swung up as gunfire spattered about. One fell dead, shot through the head. The other raiders fled down the hill toward the brush and safety leaving Crysop. I watched them gallop frantically toward the trees, flailing the horses with their reins and quirts. Just then, with a burst of motion, men and women rose up out of the grass and brush pulling the raiders from their horses, knocking them down with

277

staves and rakes. Walter England hit one man hard across the chest with the axe handle, dropping him on his back. In moments the valley was quiet. Our neighbors came out of the woods dragging the Crysop gang. Up the hill where the shots had come from, three men with guns came toward us. The first man was Ned Frolley, the sinister moonshiner. He sat his gun down, picked up Rhea, and carried her to the house. Frolley's men took the gun I had on Crysop and dragged him to his feet. He was blind, I guess, at least partway; but he was still full of hell and tried to fight them. I untied Hillary, and we went to Rhea. Frolley had taken her to the parlor. She was listening to Frolley when we came in.

"We've been keeping an eye out for you," he said. "My twin boys set up there on the hill everyday. Walter or I watch at night. The plan was Walter England's. Once the boys saw any trouble one ran for him and the other neighbors that way, and one for me and my other boys. Walter wanted us not to kill 'em if we could help it. Just shoot to scare 'em toward him and the others. We ran the raiders right into their arms, just like Walter said. For a quiet man that Walter's a good thinker."

Rhea smiled and touched Frolley's arm. "Thank you, Mr. Frolley. I thought we weren't going to make it. I was about ready to quit."

"Ma'am, you'd have died first," Frolley said. "We all owe you too much to let that happen. You rest up now and get well for Crysop's trial. We all look forward to the hanging."

Crysop never came to trial as things turned out. He escaped to become a fugitive outlaw in the West. But he never came back to Arkansas.

Hillary nursed Rhea back to health, but the real healing came with Jamie Dameron's return. He never left her again. After a while Claudia married and moved away to Baltimore. She left Joey with the Damerons. Rhea and Jamie raised us all—three orphans and their own natural daughter. They educated us and saw we had the tools for life. If we became productive men and women, it was because of them. Sarah became one of the first women to pass the Arkansas bar. Joey became a big farmer like his father, Joseph Isaacs, had wanted to be. He wore his father's watch that Rhea had saved for him after the battle. I went on to medical school and got the papers saying I was a doctor. But Rhea Dameron made me a doctor and taught me

279

many other things. When I came home I married Jessamyn Dameron, Rhea's daughter, my happiness.

We live at Vineyard together now—a family, by blood and pain and love. And at night sometimes I remember the time that brought us together, the time of the Brothers' War.

THE END